Alice
Twisted Tales of Familiar Faces
Audrey Brice

M4L Publishing

For my readers, who without, I am without.

ALICE

I STOOD ALMOST INVISIBLE against the backdrop of Willow's Edge, my presence as unremarkable as the clouds in the sky. The town itself was a pocket of seclusion, wrapped in a forest and tucked away in a corner of the world few knew existed. At thirteen years old, almost fourteen, I wore a crisp blue dress to satisfy my mother, its hue a stark contrast to the verdant spring garden and the forest beyond it. My long blonde hair fell in waves down my back, catching the sunlight in a golden cascade that framed my smooth, round face. I was quite magnificent, really. Probably the prettiest and smartest girl in all the eighth grade.

I had a secret, though. One that pulsed with a life all its own, hidden from the prying eyes of our neighbors.

Today, I stood at the edge of the forest, my breathing revealing my anticipation, my heart pounding with an intoxicating rhythm. I crouched low to the ground, my fingers stained crimson, a startling blemish on my otherwise pristine appearance. Before me lay the evidence of my macabre indulgence: two squirrels, their bodies twisted and broken, their tiny hearts silenced forever.

The first had been quick, almost too easy. I'd caught it by surprise, delighting in the frantic beating of its tiny pulse beneath my fingertips before I squeezed. There had been a brief struggle—futile, desperate scrabbling—and the crunch of tiny bone. Then, stillness. It hadn't satisfied me, though, not completely. Not like the second one.

The second squirrel had put up a fight. Its instincts had warned it of danger, and it had attempted to flee, but I was faster, more determined. The thrill of the chase had set my senses alight, every neuron firing with savage anticipation. When I finally caught it, I relished the way it writhed under my grasp, how its sharp little claws scraped against my skin in a vain attempt to escape.

I used my nails, newly manicured by my precise mother, to inflict small, calculated tears in the soft fur, watching the bright red blood well up and spill over my hands. With each piercing scream that erupted from the small creature, a shiver of pleasure cascaded down my spine. I was in control here, the master of life and death, and the power was exhilarating.

As the life drained from the second squirrel, its movements slowing until they ceased altogether, I felt a rush like no other. My chest heaved with exertion, my eyes alight with the fire of my actions and a warm sensation tingled between my legs. This was my world, my secret garden of horrors, where I was both queen and executioner.

But even as the last flutters of life left those tiny bodies, there was a pang of something else—an echo of dissatisfaction. A desire for something more, something greater. For now, though, I allowed myself to bask in the aftermath of my dark deeds, the silence of the forest an accomplice to my savagery.

"Time for lunch, Alice," came my mother's voice from the house, sweet and unsuspecting. That cow.

My eyes snapped in the direction of the sound, a mask of normalcy sliding effortlessly over my features. I stood, stepping back into the mundane world. I would need to clean this up and then wash my hands before going inside for lunch, as bloodied hands would spark questions. I picked up the dead squirrels and decided where to bury them. Yes, I knew the perfect place.

I stayed in the shadows in the back of the yard and headed toward the garden shed. When I came to the spot, I knelt on the damp earth, my pale hands working with deliberate care as I scooped out a grave beneath the dense canopy of the garden shed's forgotten corner. The soil was cool and malleable beneath my fingers, easily giving way to the shallow pit I deemed sufficient for my needs. I glanced at the lifeless bodies of the squirrels beside me, their once smooth fur now matted with crimson.

With a precision that belied my thirteen years, I wrapped each squirrel in broad leaves plucked from the surrounding underbrush, nature's shrouds concealing my macabre work from prying eyes. Then, I deposited the swaddled creatures into the ground, tucking them away like a dark secret. My heart didn't skip a beat, and my breath held steady as if this burial were but a mundane chore.

After covering the small bodies with dirt and patting it down with the flat of my hand, I gathered fallen twigs and dead leaves, scattering them over the disturbed earth to recreate a semblance of undisturbed wilderness. Not a single drop of blood remained anywhere but on my hands; my blue dress, miraculously, bore no evidence of my morning activities.

Standing back, I surveyed my work—the hidden graves now indistinguishable, in my mind at least, from the rest of the garden's unkempt edges. Satisfaction curled within me, a cold, serpentine thing that whispered praises at my cunning. But as I stared at the patch of nondescript ground, the thrill that should have bubbled in my veins felt muted, diluted by repetition and predictability.

The surrounding air seemed to still, charged with the heaviness of my thoughts. There was an itch clawing at the back of my mind, a growing hunger for a chase that wasn't over in a few heartbeats, for a prey that could look into my eyes and understand the depth of the abyss before them. These woodland creatures, they were mere playthings, too easily snuffed out to sate the gnawing emptiness inside me that yearned for something more formidable.

"More," I whispered to myself, the word a sacred vow that echoed softly amidst the trees. It was time, I knew, to seek a quarry that would invigorate my senses and challenge the sharpness of my intellect. Something that could fight, that could fear, that could truly appreciate the artistry of my dark craft.

My gaze drifted to the edge of the forest, where shadows danced with the promise of more prey scurrying just beyond sight. A rabbit, perhaps? Rabbits were cunning, quick-footed, a creature that could dart and dodge, turning the hunt into a dance of death. Yes, a rabbit would be a start, a steppingstone toward the greater aspirations that swelled within my chest.

A smile, small and secretive, toyed with the corners of my lips. The thought of pursuit, of strategy and stealth, set my heart alight with something akin to joy. I could almost taste the anticipation, sweet and heady on my tongue, as I imagined the rush of chasing down my newly chosen prey.

"Time for lunch, Alice," the call came again, closer now, and I turned, letting the mask of the dutiful daughter slip into place as seamlessly as I had concealed my violent delights.

"Coming, Mother," I replied, my voice carrying a lilt of youthful innocence. As I walked away from the garden shed and to the hose to wash my hands, my mind was already wandering through the wilds of Willow's Edge, plotting, planning, and preparing for my next hunt.

"Mother will wonder what's keeping me," I murmured to myself, wiggling my pale fingers beneath the stream of water coming from the hose. When my hands were finally clean, I turned off the spigot and shook my hands to air-dry them. I didn't want to risk wiping anything on my dress, unless I wanted my mother to have a fit. My feet carried me along the gravel path, stones crunching softly with each step as I made my way back to the house.

I approached my family's modest home, its white picket fence standing as a symbol of normalcy, but my mind danced ahead. The faces of the neighbors and community were masks I had learned to mimic, their pleasantries and small talk a language I had mastered. Every "good morning" and "how are you?" was a part of my deception.

Here I am, just Alice, I thought, stepping onto the porch where my mother stood waiting, hands on hips and a tight smile on her face.

"I called you a while ago." Her tone was slightly scolding. "Where have you been?"

"I'm sorry, Mother," I answered, my voice a melody of innocence. "The garden is looking lovelier than ever."

She looked over my shoulder into the yard beyond and shook her head ever so slightly. "Come inside. Lunch is ready. Your sister already set the table."

"Thank you, Mother," I said, offering a smile as delicate and practiced as a curtsy. As I crossed the threshold into the cool shade of the house, my bright blue eyes flickered with the thrill of my next hunt—a game only *I* knew I was playing.

I would go back out to find a rabbit after lunch.

I crouched low, my blue dress fringing the dirt as I peered through the dense shrubbery. The rabbit was there, nibbling on clover, unaware of the predator that lay in wait. I could feel the familiar tug in my chest, a yearning that was as much a part of me as the blood coursing through my veins.

"Mustn't let it control me," I murmured to myself, a mantra to quell the storm inside. My hands trembled slightly, the need for the thrill scratching at the back of my mind like a locked-away beast desperate for release. But I knew well the price of carelessness. Either I didn't catch the rabbit, or an adult caught me. I would let neither happen.

"Control," I whispered, my voice a silken thread in the quiet of the afternoon. It wasn't just about the hunt; it was about the dance of deception, the artful dodge of suspicion. A balancing act performed on the edge of a knife.

The rabbit, small and brown, twitched its nose. Caution seemed to cause the rabbit to stiffen, yet the clover was sweet, and the rabbit ignored the subtle warnings in favor of sating its hunger.

"Focus," I commanded myself, watching my prey with calculating eyes. My preparations had been precise: Over the past twenty minutes, I had observed the rabbit's habits, noted its favored patch of clover. Knowledge was my ally, diligence my weapon.

"Patience," I breathed out, willing my pulse to slow, biding my time. I had learned to wait, to let the moment ripen until it was heavy with imminent success. Only then would I strike—when the kill was assured, when no slip could betray me.

The rabbit paused, ears cocked, senses straining against the stillness. The world seemed to hold its breath, waiting for the inevitable.

Play your part, I reminded myself as I readied to pounce. This was the script I had written, the scene I had set. In this concealed stage behind my family's garden shed, I was both director and actress, the master of life and death.

The rabbit suddenly froze as if it noticed a shadow, a presence, something other than the usual rustle of leaves and the whisper of the wind.

Almost time, I thought, my heart beating a staccato rhythm against my ribs. A conflict raged within me—the hunger for more, for a challenge greater than the small bodies that lay buried beneath the earth around the shed, and a peaceful release from that hunger. I pushed the hunger down, smothered it with the same cold logic that had kept my secret safe so far.

I watched with bated breath as the rabbit twitched its nose, oblivious to the shadow of death looming just yards away. My fingers itched with anticipation, every nerve ending alight with the thrill of the imminent chase.

"Wait," I whispered to myself, the word a mantra that honed my focus.

The rabbit hopped forward, inching into the trap I had so painstakingly set. A dance as old as time, predator and prey. I drew in a deep breath. The steps had become too familiar, the rhythm too predictable.

Too easy, the thought crept in unbidden, tainting the rush of adrenaline with an edge of dissatisfaction.

The rabbit sprang into a run, too late, as I, the predator, burst forth from my cover. Every move I made was clean, practiced, leaving no trace, no clue that would lead back to the girl in the blue dress with the angelic smile. I pounced, the world blurring into streaks of green and brown as I hurtled towards my target. The rabbit bolted again, but not fast enough, not nearly fast enough to escape the fate I had crafted for it. My hands closed around its soft fur, the warmth of its life pulsing against my skin.

"Got you," I exhaled, a shudder of pleasure shaking my frame. The rabbit's panic beat against my palms, a drumroll to the climax I yearned for.

End it, the darkness inside me commanded. And I obeyed. The crack of fragile bones was a melody to my ears. My pocketknife produced a spurt of crimson before my eyes. I felt alive, every cell rejoicing in the act of extinguishing another's flame.

More, my soul cried out, even as I reveled in the rabbit's last quivering breaths. The satisfaction was fleeting, replaced by the gnawing void of unsatisfied hunger. These small creatures could no longer fill the gaping chasm within me. They were mere appetizers when I craved a feast.

I wondered then what the rabbit had thought before the darkness of death descended upon it. Perhaps it was only one word. *Escape*.

When it was over, I frowned at the anti-climax of it all. I longed for something that would test my skills, make my heart race with uncertainty and fear. The squirrels, the birds, the rabbits—they were all too simple, too weak.

Armed with a garden trowel, I picked up my fresh kill to bury it. This time, I went further back into the forest. Rabbits needed bigger graves. As I covered the freshly turned soil, erasing my steps, and cleansing my hands, I let out a heavy, dissatisfied sigh. "This is who you are," I told myself.

I stood, knowing my dark deeds would remain hidden beneath the earth. As I walked back home, my mother's voice carried through the air, calling me to dinner.

"Coming!" I called back, my voice deceptively cheerful. I put the trowel away and brushed the remnants of death from my dress. There was an art to this—the killing. It required grace and intelligence, qualities I possessed in abundance. But above all, it demanded control. Without it, I was no better than the beasts I hunted.

"Tomorrow," I promised the oncoming darkness. "Tomorrow is another day."

As I stepped through the back door, the smell of fresh bread and soup greeted me—a mundane reprieve from the extraordinary darkness that clung to me. My mother and sister smiled at me, oblivious to the monster who sat at their table. My sister, I kind of liked—even if she could be annoying. My mother, however, was smothering.

"Everything all right, dear?" she asked, sensing perhaps a flicker of something amiss.

"Perfect, Mother," I replied.

Her gray eyes settled on my dirty hands. "Wash up."

I did as I was told, returned to the table and sat in my usual spot.

My sister rolled her eyes, not making eye contact with me. We ate in a familiar, uncomfortable silence. It hadn't always been this way. Back when my father was alive, back before the darkness and the urges overcame me, we'd had lively meals with one another. We'd laugh and talk about our day and make plans for the evening or weekends. Since his death, however, the uncomfortable silence had become our pattern.

My mother had changed. Turned into the *perfect* mom, and even got a telecommute job working from home so she could spend more time with my sister and me. My sister had turned into a sullen teenager who seemed to resent family time and spent as much time on her phone as possible. Without a car, she was stuck here, just like me, unless she could convince our mom to let her go out with friends who would come pick her up.

My life was anything but normal, but we all went along, pretending like everything was okay. Everyone and everything was perfect.

The lie tasted bitter on my tongue, for perfection eluded me—it eluded us all. I ate with a fake smile on my lips, my jaw muscles pained by a practiced, pretend smile. I wondered then if my sister, even my mother, also had beasts within them. Did their beasts demand they do dark and terrible things? Did they get excited by blood and death, too? Did they want to masturbate at night after killing something helpless? The beast surfaced, the tingling between my legs began, and I wondered if it would have liked me to torture the creatures first—before I killed them.

I drew in a deep breath. "Dinner is very good tonight, Mother."

My sister groaned. "Ugh, could you make her stop that?"

"Stop what?" my mother asked.

"Calling you *Mother* and speaking like some kind of prim and proper, creepy, *Children of the Corn* type kid. It's freaking me out." My sister shot me a strange look and shivered.

I kept smiling.

"Dr. Jacobs says it's just a phase to help her cope," my mother said, then turned to me. "Isn't it, dear?"

"Yes, Mother," I replied. My plate was empty, and I was tired. "May I be excused, please?"

My mother nodded.

I went to my room and closed the door, but I could still hear my mother and sister talking.

"Come on, Mom. Something broke in her when dad died. She wears the same tatty dress every day and never lets you wash it, even though it's full of stains. She has this weird, faraway look in her eyes. She talks like a nineteenth-century posh English kid from London. It's not normal."

"Kelly," my mother started, "we need to give her time. You know how close Alice and your dad were. It's not easy for any of us," my mother began choking on her words, probably because she had begun to cry. "But it's especially hard on Alice."

"Yeah, okay," my sister said. "But I'm going to talk to Dr. Jacobs about it during my session next week."

My mother said something, but so softly I couldn't hear. I turned from the door and got undressed, changing into my nightgown. As I lay there in the dark, waiting for sleep to come, I promised the beast within that soon, very soon, I would feed it the challenge it craved. And when that day arrived, everyone would remember the name Alice, not as an unassuming teenager, but as the harbinger of their nightmares.

THE WHITE RABBIT

I NEVER IMAGINED THAT my incessant punctuality, an obsession that had become my most defining trait in Wonderland, would lead to my downfall. I, the White Rabbit, with fur as immaculate as fresh winter snow, am usually a vision of composure and nervous urgency. Now captured, as I trembled uncontrollably, my large ears twitching with every stifled heartbeat, I could barely recognize myself. The golden pocket watch that dangled from my waistcoat swung like a pendulum, marking each second of my newfound captivity.

"Please," I stammered, my voice barely a whisper, "you mustn't do this."

My captor, Alice, her name alone striking terror into the stoutest of hearts as her reputation among this world's forest animals preceded her, tilted her head, regarding me with a curiosity that chilled me to the bone. My paws flailed against her iron grip, my claws scraping helplessly against skin that seemed impervious to my desperation. In her eyes, the thrill of the hunt sparkled—a gleam I'd seen countless times in the gaze of other predators.

"Struggle all you wish, Rabbit," she murmured, her voice a lullaby that belied the horror it foretold. "It only serves to make this more... intriguing."

She didn't seem fazed at all by the fact that I could speak. I could feel the rhythmic thudding of her pulse, a macabre drumbeat accompanying my frantic attempts to escape. With each passing moment, my thoughts scattered like shattered pieces of a broken clock. Time, which had always been my relentless master, now mocked me with its steady march towards what I feared to be a grisly end.

Think, Rabbit, think! I urged myself, but panic had ensnared my wit as effectively as Alice's hands had ensnared my form. There was no burrow to dive into, no dark corner in which to vanish. There was only the cold, hard reality of her looming presence and the suffocating scent of blood that seemed to cling to her like a perverse perfume.

The press of her fingers tightened, and a wild thought ignited in my mind. "Alice," I gasped, the name cutting through the fog of fear. "There are... others. Others who are far more enticing than a mere rabbit like me."

Her grip faltered, just perceptibly. In that sliver of hesitation, I glimpsed my chance. "Wonderland," I continued, breathless with the effort to sound composed, "is a cornucopia of marvels—and horrors. Why settle for a rabbit when you could have a queen?"

"Go on," she prompted, a sly edge to her voice. I knew then that this murderess wanted a challenge.

"Targets," I said, seizing upon the word like a lifeline. "You crave more challenging prey, yes?" I didn't wait for an answer. "The Mad Hatter—his madness eclipses reason. His mind is a riddle wrapped in chaos. And the Queen of Hearts—her cruelty knows no bounds. They would be worthy of your talents as a hunter." A sly grin slid onto my lips as I realized this horrific child—this murderer—could be the answer to my prayers and those of all the inhabitants of Wonderland. *We could be rid of the cruelty and insanity once and for all.*

"Challenging prey," Alice mused, as if tasting the words. "Tell me, Rabbit, why should I trust you?"

"Because," I said, my survival instincts sharpening my tongue, "I seek an end to their tyranny as much as you seek your next thrill. We are but two sides of the same coin, you and I."

"Interesting," she whispered, almost to herself. I could see she was thinking about it, intrigued by my offer.

"Imagine it," I urged, embellishing the truth with a hint of promise, hoping to pique her interest enough that she would let me live. "A place where the impossible is commonplace, where every corner hides a secret, every shadow a story. There are creatures there that defy imagination, and all are ripe for the hunt."

"Curiouser and curiouser," she said, her tone light, yet I could feel the weight of her calculation. "You paint a vivid picture, White Rabbit."

"Only because it's true," I insisted, my heart pounding with the prospect of freedom—or doom. "Together, we could reshape Wonderland."

"Could we now?" Her eyes narrowed, assessing, and I knew this was the precipice upon which my fate teetered.

"Indeed," I said, my voice steady despite the tremor of uncertainty within. "But you'll never know unless you take the leap down the rabbit hole."

She merely stared at me, that creepy child. That murderer.

"Indeed," I said again, trying to deflect her gaze. The offer hung between us like a tantalizing fruit just out of reach. I knew if I could get back home, I could free myself from her, and I didn't really care if she murdered her way through half of Wonderland as long as she spared me. "Wonderland is not a child's playground, Alice. It is an ecosystem of the most peculiar and resilient beings. Creatures you could chase for days, mysteries that would puzzle even your sharpened mind."

Her grip on my waistcoat loosened ever so slightly, the subtle shift in her posture betraying her intrigue. I pressed on because I knew madness when I saw it, "Imagine the jubilation, the adrenaline, the ecstasy of the conquest when you outwit a Cheshire Cat that can vanish or bring down a Jabberwocky with claws that could shred the very fabric of reality."

"Interesting," she murmured again. Through her eyes, I saw Wonderland anew—not the enchanting homeland I knew, but a hunting ground teeming with danger. Enough to satiate a bloodthirsty young woman for days.

"Powerful targets, you say?" Alice's voice was laced with skepticism, and the corners of her lips twitched as if toying with the idea. "My current prey... they've become mundane, predictable. There's no reward in dispatching the defenseless."

I nodded, choosing my words with care. "In Wonderland, the prey is anything but defenseless. They are cunning, fierce, and some wield powers beyond understanding. You, Alice, would be the apex predator there—the challenge you crave, it awaits."

She appeared to ponder this, the cold gleam in her eye softening with the prospect of new obstacles. I sensed the scales tipping, my life still hanging in delicate balance. "Taking lives here has lost its savor," she confessed, a hint of weariness touching her otherwise impassive facade. "The same screams, the same deaths... It's tiresome."

"Then let me offer you respite," I proposed, desperate to seize this sliver of opportunity. "In Wonderland, your talents would be tested, your bloodlust satiated with every unpredictable move."

"Unpredictable moves..." she echoed thoughtfully, her gaze drifting past me as she undoubtedly imagined a myriad of possibilities.

"Please, Alice," I urged, my voice tremulous with the earnestness of a creature cornered. "My offer is genuine. Time is of the essence—for both of us."

Her grip on my fur loosened ever so slightly, but the threat lingered in her eyes. "And if I find this Wonderland lacking?" she asked, a dangerous edge to her question.

"Then my life is forfeit," I conceded, my heart thundering against my rib cage. "But I assure you, it will exceed your... appetites."

I watched as Alice's mind churned behind those cold, calculating eyes. Her fingers traced the outline of my waistcoat. She lifted my pocket watch and looked at the time. *Why wouldn't she hurry and make her choice?*

"Your urgency intrigues me, Rabbit," she mused, almost to herself. "What do you fear more? My knife, or what awaits back in this place you call Wonderland?"

"Both hold terrors," I admitted freely. "But only one offers you a feast for your senses—the other, a mere morsel."

A flicker of something—curiosity, perhaps—crossed her face, and I know my words had finally found their mark. She leaned closer, her breath a whisper against my whiskers. "Tell me again, White Rabbit, why should I trust you? All this could be a ruse to save your own skin."

"Because, Alice," I said, layers of truth woven into my plea, "you are a hunter, and it is in your nature to seek the most rewarding hunt. Wonderland is not a lie—it is the untamed wild, where prey fights back with tooth and claw. You would not be bored there."

She contemplated this some more, her gaze distant yet sharp. With every second that passed, I felt the balance slowly shift, as she wavered on the brink of decision.

"Venturing into the unknown, chasing shadows that may bite back..." Alice's voice trailed off. "It's tempting, Rabbit. Very tempting."

"Then take the leap, Alice," I said. "Let Wonderland challenge you. Let it fuel your desires."

"Or let it be my downfall," she countered, though I detected a tremor of excitement beneath her words.

"Life without risk is no life at all," I said, jumping on that moment of her vulnerability. "You crave more than this mundane existence—you hunger for a game worthy of your skill."

Alice stood silent; the internal struggle etched upon her face. A predator poised on the precipice of an entirely new hunting ground, torn by the allure of the chase and the shadow of uncertainty.

"Decide, Alice," I pushed gently. "Your destiny, my fate—they await your verdict."

A slow, deliberate nod signaled the end of her contemplation. "Very well, White Rabbit," she said, and with those words, I felt the chains of my impending doom loosen. She let me go and slipped the knife back into her dress pocket. "Lead the way."

I paused, unsure if I should lead her to Wonderland, or if I should make a run for it and hope she didn't catch me again. On one hand, the death of the Queen and the Mad Hatter would make my life more peaceful, but didn't that make me every bit as bloodthirsty as Alice? All the animals in the forest knew about her. They'd heard the agonizing screams of those that had fallen victim to her. These stories had traveled all the way to Wonderland. Because of this, I had known better than to venture topside, but I was late and had an appointment. Tea with the Hatter, actually. So, I'd taken the chance and been caught. Now, I could simply allow her to kill me, or risk being seen as her co-conspirator. I didn't want to die.

"Lead the way, Rabbit," she repeated, her voice steadier now, each syllable a hammer strike sealing the pact.

I let out a sigh of relief, but my large ears still quivered as I turned toward the gaping maw of my rabbit hole that led to safety and darkness.

Alice followed, talking to herself all the while. "Into the abyss then," she said, the words more breath than sound. With each step towards the opening in the ground, my heart quickened.

"Be wary, Alice," I told her as we descended into the earth, my voice an eerie lullaby in the encroaching gloom. "Wonderland can be unkind to the uninitiated."

She smirked at my warning; her gaze locked on the descending darkness. "Kindness is not a language I speak, dear Rabbit," she said, her eyes glinting with feral glee. "It's the cruelty, the madness of your world that calls to me."

My eyes met hers and for a moment, despite the blueness of her eyes, it felt like twin pools of midnight reflecting back at me. "Then you shall have your fill," I whispered, and with those words, we plunged into the rabbit hole together.

I made it down the tunnel first just fine, but I could hear the girl brushing the walls of the passage. She was far too big, which meant I could have easily outrun her if I'd wanted to, but something kept me from running.

"Remember, Alice," I said as she fell, "the creatures of Wonderland are not like what you have faced before. They think, they fight." I suppose, in repeating this, I hoped it would discourage her. It didn't.

"Let them come," she said. "I am no stranger to monsters."

Alice hit the ground with a thud, an abrupt end to her plunge down the rabbit hole. The fall seemed to have knocked the air from her lungs.

"Welcome to Wonderland," I said.

She lifted herself and looked around at my tiny home, in which she was far too big. She couldn't rise to her feet, which meant she couldn't chase me. "Where are the monsters you assured me would be here?" she asked, the hunter within already seeking her prey.

"Patience, Alice," I said, dusting off my waistcoat. "They are closer than you think."

She tried to rise again, but she gave up when her head hit the ceiling. "How am I supposed to..."

I went over to one cabinet along the wall. Alice's size wouldn't do. Taking out a bottle labeled *shrink*, I handed it to her. "You'll need to drink this."

With two fingers, she took the bottle from me and removed the cork, eyeing it suspiciously. "How do I know it's not poison?"

Alice was a smart human, indeed. "Read the label," I said.

"Shrink," she said.

"Yes, you need to be smaller to enter wonderland."

Her face twisted into frustration. "You didn't tell me I would have to become small!"

"You wanted a challenge, did you not?"

She glowered at me momentarily, then, out of what felt like sheer spite, downed the bottle's contents. Nothing happened immediately. But then, a surprised look filled her eyes, and the bottle dropped to the ground. Rather quickly, she began to shrink and let out a small yelp. I was sure I saw a glimmer of fear in her eyes that wonder quickly replaced. She held her hands out in front of her, looked at me at eye level, and then a peculiar grin slid over her lips. "My clothes have shrunk, too." Reaching her hand into her pocket, she pulled out the knife, which had also shrunk. "Curiouser and curiouser," she said.

"Indeed," I said. With her and me more evenly matched, I could outrun her now if I wanted to or fight her off with my powerful back legs. But I didn't. I wanted to see this through. See if the vicious killer before me had the strength to survive Wonderland when the creatures weren't so much smaller than she was. See if she could rid us of our volatile queen most of all.

"Come now," I told her. "Your prey awaits." I gestured to my small front door leading into the wide world of Wonderland.

Alice walked past me to the door, as if I no longer existed. Anticipation covered her youthful face. She pulled it open and stepped out into the bright sunlight of the forest.

I followed, closing the door to my den behind us.

As if on cue, a low growl resounded through the trees, a sound so primal it set her instincts aflame. She jumped and took out her knife while I stayed behind. I knew what those sounds belonged to. A shadow flitted between the darkened trunks, too quick for her eyes to follow. Another joined it, and then another, until an orchestra of snarls and rustling leaves surrounded us.

"Be ready," I warned, my ears twitching in every direction. "Wonderland's welcome committee is here."

I saw her bristle with anticipation. Her fingers curled into fists, almost eager to meet the challenge head-on. She took a step forward, the queer smile on her lips a silent dare to the creatures hidden within the shadows.

"Let them come," she whispered.

And just as the first creature leaped from the darkness, its eyes glinting with malice, Alice turned toward it. The line between hunter and hunted blurred, and I imagined in her mind that the question that lingered was: Who truly was the predator, and who was the prey?

"Are you frightened, Alice?" I asked, my voice steady, knowing that I was in little danger having spent my entire life in this place.

"Terrified," she lied, her grin betraying the truth of her yearning.

"Do you think you're going mad?" I asked, more insidious this time.

A sly grin slid over her lips. "Aren't we all mad here?"

ALICE

THE RABBIT'S OFFER WAS intriguing, so I followed, and the earth yawned open beneath us. I could sense the White Rabbit's trepidation as much as my own. Darkness enveloped us, a shroud that blurred the edges of reality. My feet lost touch with the ground; were we falling—or were we flying? I couldn't tell. The Rabbit's coat brushed against my arm, real and solid amidst the surreal tumble through the dark space. But then the Rabbit disappeared, and I found myself alone.

"Curiouser and curiouser," I murmured to myself, echoing words I'd spoken before in a dream that was now my reality. The walls of the rabbit hole bent and contorted, stretching into infinity, defying logic and physics. I was no longer anchored to the world above, and with each passing second, my former life faded like a distant echo.

I could feel it, too, the pull of the otherworldly vortex swallowing us whole. It should have been terrifying, but there was an exhilarating freedom in the descent, in my surrender to forces beyond my control.

I exchanged a few words with the Rabbit that I immediately forgot as I hit the ground with a thud; the air pushed from my lungs on impact. I regained my composure and found myself in a small and confined space that I barely fit into.

The Rabbit stood a few feet away, watching me with interest. It was no longer afraid of me because it knew I couldn't chase or get hold of it here. There wasn't enough room. I felt frustration build inside me. "Where are the monsters you assured me would be here?"

"Patience, Alice," he said, dusting off his waistcoat. "They're closer than you think."

I tried to rise, but my head hit the soft dirt above. "How am I supposed to…"

The Rabbit went over to a rabbit-sized cabinet along the wall and produced a bottle, handing it to me and urging me to drink it. It was so small that I could only grab it with two fingers.

My eyes burned into him for a moment. What if it was poison? The bottle was small enough. But if it were poison, there likely wasn't enough there to kill me. The Rabbit drew my attention to the label on the bottle, which read *Shrink*. He insisted I'd need to shrink if I wanted to enter Wonderland. For a moment, I felt angry; the Rabbit hadn't been upfront with me. But as I was already here and there was no point going back, I removed the cork, put the mouth of the bottle to my lips, and threw my head back. It tasted bitter, whatever it was.

Just when I thought it wasn't working, I felt a strange sensation in my stomach that spread outward to the rest of my body, and suddenly, I felt like I was falling again. I let out a small yelp, but as soon as it had started, it was over and I was barely taller than the Rabbit, and the Rabbit was bulkier than I. Holding my hands in front of me, everything appeared normal. Even my dress still fit. "My clothes have shrunk, too," I said. Then I remembered my pocketknife. Reaching into my pocket, I felt the cool steel and took it out, opening the blade. "Curiouser and curiouser," I said.

"Indeed," said the Rabbit. "Come now, your prey awaits." With an outstretched paw, he motioned me toward a door.

I walked past the Rabbit and to the door, my heart pounding with unbridled anticipation. Pulling it open, I stepped into the bright sunlight. When we emerged from the Rabbit's den, it was as though we'd been born into a kaleidoscope. Wonderland greeted me with an explosion of color, the sky a canvas painted by a mad artist. Purples and pinks clashed and blended with blues that swirled like whirlpools overhead. My breath caught in my throat as I marveled at the beauty, at the sheer vibrancy that saturated every inch of this place the White Rabbit called Wonderland.

A low growl came from the left. Something wild and dangerous was coming, so I took my knife and held it in front of me. A dark shadow raced between the underbrush, though I couldn't see what it was. It was too fast. Another unseen creature joined the first, and then another, until snarls and movement surrounded us.

"Be ready," the Rabbit said from behind me. "Wonderland's welcome committee is here."

I balled my fist, my right hand gripping the knife, and got ready. This would certainly be a challenge. "Let them come," I whispered.

And just as the first creature leaped from the darkness, its eyes bugging and bulging, I turned toward it.

"Are you frightened, Alice?" the Rabbit asked. I sensed a bit of hope in his voice.

"Terrified," I deadpanned, grinning ear to ear.

"Do you think you're going mad?" the Rabbit asked, this time more boldly.

I smiled, wondering what the Rabbit's game was. Sure, this place was strange, but nothing I couldn't handle. Was the furry beast attempting to make me think I was going crazy? A response popped into my head, and I blurted it out, "Aren't we all mad here?"

A large grasshopper flew at me, and I dove to the ground before realizing that these large insects weren't attacking—they were simply jumping over us. They weren't growling either. It was just a strange noise they made. Twenty of them, at least. They surrounded us, their weird buggy eyes filled with what I could only describe as curiosity.

"Remarkable, isn't it?" The White Rabbit's voice came from behind me, yet there was an undercurrent of something else—caution, perhaps, or the burden of some knowledge that I was not yet privy to.

"Indeed," I said, unable to tear my gaze from the spectacle all around me. "It's like nothing I've ever seen."

The Rabbit stepped up next to me and we stood, side by side, two figures dwarfed by the splendor of Wonderland, and for a fleeting moment, I wondered if I was meant to find this place, or if it found me. Regardless, the colors beckoned, promising wonders and horrors alike.

The giant grasshoppers glanced at one another, seemingly satisfied that we belonged here, then with powerful hind legs, they leapt away and disappeared back into the forest.

"Come now," the Rabbit said, leading me down a cobbled path into the forest and who knew where. "We have an appointment." He glanced at his pocket watch. "We're already late."

I had no choice but to follow. The ground beneath my boots quivered as if the very earth of Wonderland resented my intrusion. I couldn't help but marvel at the grotesqueness that skittered across our path; creatures with too many eyes, too many limbs, all moving in a discordant dance of life so alien to my own. My fingers remained curled around the handle of my blade—an extension of my will, a silent partner in my hunt.

"Such oddities," I murmured.

A flower turned its bloom towards us, its petals vibrating with the intensity of its verbal sparring with the neighboring flora. The colors were vivid, almost violently so, and for a moment, their savage beauty enthralled me. It must have been the stench of the upper world on my skin that called to the denizens of this place, because it was as if these strange creatures had come out of their way to cross our path.

"Careful, Alice," the White Rabbit warned from beside me as if he had been reading my mind, his whiskers twitching with unease. "They can smell the foreignness on you."

The ground rumbled, and an army of giant rats emerged from the underbrush, teeth bared, eyes glinting with malevolence. For the first time, I realized that in this world, I could be mistaken for an easy meal. One rat lunged, a blur of fur and fangs, but I was quicker. I thrust my blade forward, finding the rat's jugular with ease. Blood bloomed from its neck and the creature fell, causing its kin to retreat into the shadows. I examined the twitching creature as it died.

"Efficient," I said dryly, wiping my blade clean on the fallen beast's fur.

"Disturbingly so," the Rabbit replied. His paw reached for the pocket watch again. It appeared to be a nervous tic that spoke volumes about his comfort, or lack thereof, in my presence.

"Where, exactly, do you have to be?" I asked.

The White Rabbit hesitated, then said, "A tea party."

"Okay." My eyes narrowed as I stared the Rabbit down. "Really? A tea party?"

"We're going to see the Mad Hatter," the Rabbit said with a quiver in his voice.

"Why is he called the Mad Hatter?" I asked.

"You will know once you meet him," the Rabbit assured me.

My gaze shifted beyond the carnage I had inflicted on the rat, and we continued along the path. Finally, from the winding path, we came to a clearing. There sat a table set for a tea party. The bright yellow table had mismatched green and red chairs and several orange and blue teapots spewing steam. The clearing suddenly erupted into chaos when a figure in a top hat grander than any crown I'd ever imagined entered the garden with a prancing cat at his heels.

"The Mad Hatter," I whispered, feeling the pulse in my veins quicken. Rats were one thing, but a person, much like me, was a new challenge that sent a thrill through me as anticipation coiled in my stomach like a snake ready to strike.

"His mind is a puzzle wrapped in a paradox, as I've always said," the Rabbit whispered back, though I barely heard him over the rush of blood in my ears.

"Perfect," I said.

"Be wary, Alice. He is not what he seems," the Rabbit said, but the wind carried away his words. I was already moving toward the tea party, my senses alight.

"Ah, there you are! You're late!" the Hatter cried, looking past me to the White Rabbit. "But time is of no matter. It goes backwards and forwards and sometimes it sits still. As the sun is in the sky always and never there." Then, the Hatter noticed me. "You brought a friend."

I stopped in my tracks, still clutching the knife.

The Rabbit cleared his throat. "This is Alice," he said

The Hatter briefly removed his hat and bowed. "Welcome, Alice. Will you have some tea?"

I was caught off guard by the question, for none of my prey had ever asked if I sought refreshment.

The Rabbit hopped ahead and sat at the table, glancing at me, then at the Hatter, then back at me. The strange smiling cat jumped onto the violet picket fence on one side of the garden, making me realize there was a house there that almost blended into the forest backdrop. "Curiouser and curiouser," I muttered beneath my breath, slipping the knife back into my dress pocket.

"I have gumdrop, turquoise, and daisy green," the Hatter said, motioning to the teapots. "And dandelion cakes, too."

Stunned, I moved to the table and sat down. I could only imagine what the Rabbit must have thought about me then. I was supposed to kill this Hatter, not engage in some strange chaotic tea party.

"Good, good." The Hatter gave me a small plate with a dandelion cake on it and poured me some gumdrop tea. Then he served the Rabbit and an empty chair before serving himself. Finally, he sat. "Drink up, drink up! The tea will get cold."

I sipped the tea, surprised it tasted like cherry gumdrops.

"So, what do you do, Alice?"

"Do?" I asked. No one had ever asked me that before. I giggled, my mind screaming, *In the summer months, I visit Wonderland to kill Mad Hatters.* Instead, I said, "I'm traveling at the moment."

"Oh, how lovely! You should attend the Queen's croquet party while you're here. Hear. Here. I love words that are the same but different." He smiled at the White Rabbit. "And what have you been up to, my furry friend?"

I could see the Rabbit bristle. He grabbed his pocket watch and glanced at it again. "The usual."

"Hmm." Then the Hatter looked at the empty chair. "Indeed," he said. "More people should mock those mockingbirds. So annoying."

A smile slipped over my lips unbidden. Perhaps I had met my match, for the Mad Hatter was certainly madder than me.

The Mad Hatter continued with this nonsensical conversation with the chair for a few more minutes, until finally, his gaze settled on me again. "What is your direction?"

"My direction?"

"I much prefer up south!" He shouted this as if it were a revelation.

I thought about arguing with him that up south wasn't a direction, but then realized it would be futile to argue with someone who was crazy. "You're absolutely insane."

The Hatter's white gloved hand went to his chest as if I'd just offended him. "Are you suggesting I'm mad?"

That sly grin returned to my lips. "Well, you are the Mad Hatter, but you're not as mad as I am."

He leaned back in his chair and gave the Rabbit an odd look. "What is the meaning of this?"

I drew his attention back to me by standing. "The Rabbit has nothing to do with this. It's between you and me. I'm here to kill you." I regretted saying it the second the words left my lips. Now, the Hatter would have time to flee, and I no longer had the edge. At the same time, it would require me to hunt him. My heart began thumping in my chest and I took up my knife again, opening it.

"I beg your pardon?" he asked. His body stiffened. Even the messy orange hair beneath his jaunty hat seemed to freeze.

My grin widened. "Today, Wonderland will remember the true meaning of madness," I said. "And it will wear my face."

The Hatter jumped up and made a run for the woods.

I joined in the chase. The terrain twisted around us, a labyrinth of grotesque hedges and gnarled trees. The Mad Hatter's silhouette flitted ahead, his coattails flapping like the wings of a deranged crow. My breath came in ragged gasps, not from exertion but exhilaration. Every bounding step brought me closer to my quarry. Every thorn that scratched at my arms was a love bite from Wonderland itself.

He glanced back, eyes wide with a concoction of fear and madness, and my lips curled upward. His terror perfumed the air. I vaulted over a fallen log while my heart sang a violent hymn.

"Run, Hatter, run," I called out to him.

The Mad Hatter zigzagged, then out of nowhere, he began throwing strange obstacles in my path that seemed to materialize out of thin air. Teacups the size of boulders rolled towards me, spilling rivers of scalding tea. I danced around them, nimble, my blade glinting in the ever-changing light. He was clever, this one, but desperation made his movements predictable.

Closer still, I drew, the gap between us narrowing until I could see the individual threads fraying at the brim of his hat. I inhaled deeply the scent of sweat and gumdrop tea.

I knew in that moment he'd realized the futility of his flight. His shoulders slumped, the fight seeping out of him. There he was, cornered against a backdrop of bleeding hearts and cackling roses. His back turned to me once more, resignation etched into his trembling frame. I closed in, each step a silent drumroll to the finale.

"End of the line, Hatter," I said, my voice low and triumphant. My hand rose, the blade catching the light, a beacon of the end times for this mad, mad man.

"Time for tea," I said, just before plunging the knife into the side of his neck, right through the carotid artery, into the ecstasy of the hunt's end. Blood spurted from the man's neck as he fell to his knees, clutching at the wound as if that would stop the crimson flow of his life from draining away. Finally, he fell forward and stopped moving.

THE WHITE RABBIT

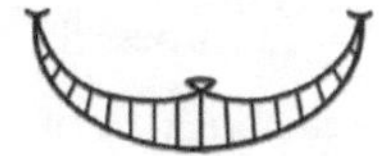

FROM BEHIND THE SAFETY of a gnarled tree, I observed with wide eyes. My paws trembled. Alice had changed into a bloodthirsty predator. She stood over the still form of the Mad Hatter, watching the last of his blood leak from the gaping wound in his neck. I swallowed hard. That could have just as easily been me lying there.

"Madness," I muttered to myself, realizing too late the gravity of my mistake. It wasn't just the life of a rat, or of the Hatter—it was all of Wonderland in danger. Me included. Her insatiable hunger could destroy us all. Regret was a stone in my gut, heavy and immovable. I took a step back, my whiskers quivering with the shock of my realization. What had I done? By guiding Alice here, I had unleashed a beast, and the reflection in the looking glass no longer showed a curious girl but a harbinger of doom.

"Forgive me," I whispered, though there was no one to hear me. The surrounding forest had gone silent, and the shadows seemed to lean in closer, as if they, too, knew the cost of my folly.

Alice turned to me. "We should finish our tea. At least now we won't have to listen to his mad rambling." Then Alice walked past me, back toward the Hatter's house and the waiting tea party.

I followed with some reluctance. I could control her for now, but how long before I had no hold over her? Now, I had to find a way to distract her and to send her back to her world before she could do more damage.

"How did he magically create huge teacups to throw in my path?" Alice asked once we'd sat back down at the table.

I could see her brain fervently working on the mystery, as if she were pondering finding a way to harness the magic of Wonderland for herself. That would have been another grave mistake.

"Shrinking potions, manifesting things that weren't there before. It's like magic," she said, echoing my private thoughts.

"The potion comes from a plant, but I dare say I don't know how the Mad Hatter had the power to throw large teacups in your path," I said, hoping my face didn't betray my lie. I knew damn well how the Hatter had done it. It *was* magic.

She nodded, as if accepting my explanation. She ate two of the dandelion cakes, and then, much to my relief, she yawned. "I'm so tired."

My heart leapt with hope. "You must rest then. Go now into the Hatter's house where you can sleep and I shall keep watch out here," I said, hoping my suggestion wouldn't cause suspicion.

Alice stretched her arms out and yawned again. "Yes. That sounds nice."

She got up and disappeared around the side of the Hatter's house and went inside. I heard the door close behind her.

My eyes darted around the clearing, then to the violet picket fence, a favorite perching spot for the Cheshire Cat. "Cat," I called ever so softly. "Where have you gone?"

There was movement on the far side of the garden, so I hopped toward it to investigate.

"Here, here," I heard a voice say.

I followed it into a thicket and found myself face to face with the Cheshire Cat, a wide grin on his feline lips.

"You brought the dangerous creature here," the Cat said. It wasn't a question.

Looking down, ashamed of my arrogance in thinking I could control Alice, I only nodded.

"Why?"

The Cat's stare made me shift uncomfortably in its gaze. "She caught me topside and would have killed me had I not promised her a more fruitful hunt here. I thought..." I paused, not wanting to admit my want for selfish gain from Alice's bloodlust.

"You thought?" the Cat asked, urging me to finish the thought.

"I thought she could rid us of the Hatter and the Queen and then I would find a way to send her back to her world and make her big again so she could never come back." Just saying the words caused my stomach to flip with unease. How could I have been so foolish?

"It's a conundrum," the Cat said, still smiling. That was the thing about the Cheshire Cat. One could never really tell how he felt about anything. He usually spoke in riddles, but today, he was rather direct, which jarred me.

"Can you help me?"

The Cheshire Cat leaned into me, his nose almost touching mine. "We should also rid our land of Tweedledee and Tweedledum. Wonderland has no use for such oafs."

I blinked back my surprise. "They're harmless, though."

"It is sought by all, yet found by few. In silence and in calm, it dwells true. It bridges the gaps, ends the fights. In its presence, hearts feel light," the Cat said, pulling away from me. But his eyes didn't leave mine and that wide smile didn't falter.

I smiled, taking in his words. This was the Cat I knew; one that spoke in riddles.

The Cat gave me an expectant look.

"I don't know what your riddle means. To end the fighting?" I tried.

"Peace!" He let out an exasperated sigh. "A peaceful Wonderland is but a dream."

"Will you assist me or not?"

The Cat sat back on his haunches. "Very well. But only if we remove the Tweedles."

"Fine." I needed the Cat—a master of space and time—to deal with Alice. A noise came from the direction of the Hatter's house, then the door closed.

"Rabbit?" came Alice's voice.

The Cat's grin grew wider and in a bright flash of light, he vanished. I instinctively hid, even though I knew I would have to face her. The thumping of my own panicked heartbeat was the only sound that dared to break the eerie silence. Regret clenched within me, its venomous grip tightening with each breath I drew.

I watched her, this girl, barely a woman, with innocent blonde locks and eyes as sharp as the Jabberwocky's talons. Alice wove her way between the gnarled trees, past the Cheshire Cat's favorite perch—now empty, save for the lingering memory of his vanishing grin.

"Come out, come out," Alice sang softly, a siren's lullaby that held no charm but a chilling promise of things to come. "White Rabbit," Alice called again, her voice slicing through the stillness. "Where have you gone?"

Finally, I appeared from my hiding place, faking a yawn and stretching. "I'm here," I said.

"Sleeping?" She put her hands on her hips, her blue and white dress now marred with splattered, dried blood.

"Yes," I said, looking around to see if any other creatures hid nearby. It was best to lead her onward, away from here, so the Cheshire Cat could come up with his plan. In the meantime, I would take her to the Tweedles to pay the cat's price, and then to the Queen, in order to fully complete my own twisted desire for peace. If the Cat kept his word, then it would all be over. I vowed then and there to never travel topside again. "Come, we should go," I said quickly.

I led her away from the now quiet clearing where the Mad Hatter's home and body lay, into the forest, along the path. The air, fragrant with flowers and sweet scents I usually enjoyed, now smelled rancid. I didn't take a direct route, hoping the twists and turns in our path would confuse Alice so she wouldn't be able to find her way back to revisit her conquests, but more importantly, so that she could never find my home again.

I hopped quietly ahead, only glancing back occasionally to make sure she was following. Her eyes, filled with wonder, darted in all directions and toward every sound. I could tell she had never seen such creatures as those we passed, or those that flew overhead. Thankfully, she didn't appear to want to violently maim every living thing that crossed our path. After a few minutes, the trail cleared and ahead sat a caterpillar on a mushroom.

Both Alice and I stopped in our tracks.

"I've never seen one so big," Alice said, her eyes wide.

"Who are you?" The Caterpillar's languid form uncoiled atop the mushroom cap. He regarded both Alice and me with an air of detached curiosity, oblivious to the evil that Alice carried in her heart.

Alice stepped forward. "I'm Alice. This is the White Rabbit. Who are you?"

The Caterpillar regarded her for a moment. "I'm the one all creatures come to when they seek wisdom."

"But you're a caterpillar," she said, her face contorting with confusion.

"And you are human," he replied.

I wanted to scream out, to warn him of the malevolence that lurked behind Alice's fair facade, but I simply froze and glanced at each of them, unsure what to expect.

Alice, however, seemed uninterested in disemboweling the Caterpillar. At least for now. "We're just traveling through," she said.

My heart thrummed in my chest, my paws digging into the dirt beneath them.

"Do you know your way?" the Caterpillar asked. "Where you're going, I mean."

Her eyes turned to me. "The Rabbit knows," she said, but then something in her eyes changed and they narrowed. "Though maybe you can tell me about the magic of Wonderland. How does one go from big to small? Or pull large teacups from thin air?"

The Caterpillar mused, clearly mistaking her predatory patience for genuine interest. "There are secrets to Wonderland, potions that unlock doors to realms unseen."

"Really?" Her voice lifted. "It was a potion that made me small. What about pulling large teacups from thin air?"

"I only know the way of potions." The Caterpillar extended a leg, presenting a vial filled with a dark green liquid. I wanted to jump up and grab it, but knew if I did, Alice would chase me to the ends of Wonderland to get it. "If you drink this, you could walk among us, transparent. The answers you seek might reveal themselves when viewed from the cloak of invisibility."

I gulped.

Alice's gaze settled on me. "Should I?" she asked.

Was it possible Alice saw me as an ally and not just a means to an end that she would eventually dispose of?

"I'm not sure," I said carefully.

This potion would be the key to our undoing. To gift Alice with such power was to invite a fox into the henhouse, all the while blindfolding the guards.

But Alice reached out and took the vial. "Thank you," she said.

As the vial changed hands, my heart sank. Now, I would have to find a way to keep her from drinking it.

Alice wasn't done, however. "Do you know of anyone who can teach me the magic to make things appear and disappear?"

The Caterpillar considered this for a moment, then shook his head. "The Hatter has powers like that, but I've never heard of another. That ability is likely unique to him," he said carefully.

In that moment, I thought I could sense a knowing in the Caterpillar, as if he'd been placed here on purpose to thwart Alice, and from the corner of my eye, I thought I saw the Cheshire Cat, but when I turned to look, there was nothing there.

Alice let out a sigh. "Oh well, invisibility will do," she said, slipping the vial into her dress pocket.

I breathed a hopeful sigh of relief that she didn't use the potion then and there.

"It was nice to meet you, Caterpillar, and thank you for the potion," Alice said, then she turned to me. "Lead on, Rabbit."

With a quick warning look at the Caterpillar, I hopped ahead, leading Alice further into the forest. Once we'd gotten far enough away, I stopped and turned to her, hoping my next question would help me gain more of her trust. "Do you really think you should drink that potion when the time comes?"

"Why shouldn't I?" she asked. "I drank your potion."

"My potion was normal. What if his potion is poison?" I countered. Sure, I could have been foiling the Cat's plans, but all I could think about was the danger Alice posed if she were invisible. My whiskers twitched with apprehension, my mind racing with visions of unseen terror sweeping through Wonderland. The cat's grin fading into nothingness, the Caterpillar's once wise voice made silent.

"Curiouser and curiouser," Alice murmured, pulling the vial from her pocket and rolling it between her fingers. A pause lingered between us, as if time itself held its breath, waiting for her decision. Her gaze locked onto the potion.

My mind went back to the Caterpillar. I'd seen him before. Always on a mushroom cap minding his own business, usually surrounded by smoke rings as he puffed on his pipe. He knew the Cat. This was a plan.

"I'll save it for the right time," Alice finally said, slipping the vial back into her pocket with a nod.

An invisible girl could get away with all sorts of mischief, I thought, and shuddered. I led onward, the danger of Alice clear and palpable as the evening mist crept over Wonderland. In the fading light, each step turned us into specters of malice, sowing discord. My imagination ran rampant, and I tried to focus on the path and not think about what was to come.

"I'm getting hungry," Alice said from behind me. Her voice sounded whiny, like a child's.

I immediately stopped and sniffed the wind, the slight breeze hitting my whiskers. The scent of meat pies and cakes floated by.

"What is that glorious smell?" she asked.

I knew then that we were near the Duchess's house. The Duchess was a friend, and I didn't want Alice to harm her, but I also knew this was the closest house with food in it, and that the Duchess could offer us a room for the night. The Cheshire Cat was likely already there and had, hopefully, warned the Duchess of Alice's nefarious intentions for Wonderland.

"Well," Alice said, reaching out and poking me with her finger.

I jumped. "Yes, yes. Of course. The smell of such a meal could only come from the Duchess's house. Come along, no time to waste." I pulled the pocket watch from my waistcoat and glanced at the time. "We mustn't be late." I beckoned Alice forward. There was no choice now but to trust the Cheshire Cat. Though how I would lead Alice to eliminate the Tweedles along with the Queen still eluded me. It wasn't as if we could hunt the Tweedles down or simply walk into the palace grounds uninvited.

Wonderland, however, had other ideas. Between us and the Duchess's house there was a field, and in it, on the other side of a shallow pond, were a mouse, a dodo, a lory, and an eaglet. From the excited voices, it was clear something was going on.

"What is this?" Alice asked, her eyes narrowing.

"You there—you must swim through the pool and then come to the circle," the Mouse commanded.

"But why?" Alice asked. Instead of jumping into the small pond, she merely walked around it. I followed.

"Can't you see we're getting ready to run a caucus?" The birds all nodded at the Mouse's question.

"A caucus?" Alice repeated as if the word were foreign. She eyed each of the birds hungrily. "I wonder if we should bring something to the Duchess," she said. "A gift for the hostess?"

"Oh, no," I said, my voice on the verge of a cry. These creatures were innocent. I leaned in to her and whispered in her ear, "These creatures aren't fit for eating." I made a face as if to emphasize my point.

She nodded and let out a heavy sigh. "Very well. I'm much too tired of walking and would prefer to go to the Duchess's house."

"But you must at least watch the race," the Mouse said.

"Perhaps we should indulge them," I said.

Alice nodded in agreement. "Very well, go ahead then."

In a flurry of chaos, the birds all ran in a chaotic circle until the Mouse cried, "The race is over!"

I fought the urge to roll my eyes.

"I won!" the Eaglet cried.

"No, I won," countered the Lory.

"That wasn't a race and there was no clear winner," Alice said, her eyes narrowing again. "But I'll tell you what," she pulled the knife from her dress pocket and opened it up. "Whoever can get away from me will live. The losers will die."

Before I could stop her, Alice raced forward, knife clutched in her hand, swinging wildly at the Mouse and the birds who scattered in all directions, running for their lives. She chased them all into the surrounding forest, and when she stopped, she threw her head back in hideous laughter. Then she turned to me and my blood ran cold.

"Now *that* was a race," she said with a giggle, closing the knife and slipping it back into her pocket. "Come on." This time, Alice led the way toward the scent of food, away from the clearing. As we left, I could feel the eyes of terrified creatures watching us from the forest. I didn't glance back.

It was less than a mile to the Duchess's house. We'd get there just before dark. Ahead of me, Alice skipped along like a child, humming a strange, dark melody to herself. I hopped along behind her and didn't dare breathe a word.

ALICE

THE DUCHESS'S HOUSE LOOMED eerily in front of us, the darkness encroaching on either side. The forest became a twisted, tangled maze of trees and underbrush. I could hear the strange creatures of Wonderland skittering through the darkness and could feel eyes from above boring down on us. I stopped in my tracks, hearing the Rabbit stop behind me. "How perfectly dark," I said.

"I should go ahead so I can introduce you," the Rabbit said. I could hear a slight quiver in his voice. He feared me, though I wasn't sure why. I had no desire to kill him. Not yet anyway.

My hand ventured to my dress pocket so I could pat my knife, making sure it was there and ready to go should I need it. The White Rabbit hopped ahead, and ever in a hurry, knocked briskly on the door. Almost immediately, it was flung open by one I later learned was the Cook, a tired and stern-looking woman, who greeted us with a tremendous sneeze that sent a cloud of pepper from the shaker in her hand into the air.

I pulled back. "Bless you!" I said, fully aware there was a bit of disdain in my voice. I waved my hand in front of me in a futile attempt to clear the pepper from the air. Before the Rabbit or I could say more, a small piglet darted between our legs and out the door, squealing in delight. Hot on its heels came a woman I assumed was the Duchess, her face filled with determination and annoyance. The Rabbit and I jumped to the side, otherwise she likely would have run us down.

"Come back here, you little rascal!" she cried, her voice echoing down the path as she chased after the piglet.

The Cook, seemingly unfazed by the commotion, wiped her nose with the corner of her apron and gestured for us to enter. "Come in, come in," she said gruffly, leading us into the dining room. It was almost as if we were... expected. I glanced at the Rabbit, wondering if he'd somehow called ahead, but there were no phones here. Not in Wonderland.

Then I wondered if word was out that I was here, and people had simply prepared. A rush of panic ran through me. What if news of the creatures I'd killed, including that insane Hatter, had also traveled throughout Wonderland? I narrowed my eyes at the thought.

"Alice, please sit," the Rabbit said, looking bewildered himself, as if our current situation was foretold by some unseen force.

Turning my attention to the room, I focused, and to my astonishment, the table was laden with the most extraordinary array of foods I had ever seen. There were meat pies, cakes shaped like toadstools, jellies that shimmered like rainbows, and a roast that appeared to be a hedgehog, though I dared not ask if it truly was.

The Rabbit motioned to the large men sitting at the table opposite us. Identical twins, they both wore blue pants with blue suspenders and white shirts. "Tweedledee and Tweedledum, or as we call them around here, The Tweedles," the Rabbit told me. There was a hint of annoyance in his voice.

The Tweedles did not acknowledge us because they were engaged in a heated argument.

"You're quite mistaken, brother," Tweedledee declared, pounding the table for emphasis. "Everyone knows the moon is a fine cheddar!"

"Nonsense!" retorted Tweedledum, crossing his arms. "It's a giant biscuit, and that's the end of it!"

The Rabbit and I exchanged bemused glances as we took our seats. I couldn't help but smile at the absurdity of it all. Wonderland, it seemed, never ceased to surprise me, but I decided then and there that if I was going to kill anyone this night, the Tweedles would likely be my next victims. They were incredibly annoying.

The Duchess hadn't returned, but the ridiculous argument continued, and the Cook began serving us portions of the strange feast. I took a cautious bite of a jelly that tasted of lavender and honey and found it surprisingly delightful. The meat pies were also divine. The Rabbit, meanwhile, nibbled on a piece of carrot cake that made his ears twitch with every bite.

Just as I was relaxing, the Duchess burst back into the room, the piglet now cradled in her arms. "Caught the little scamp!" she announced triumphantly, plopping the piglet onto a chair beside her. "Now, who's going to go with me tomorrow to play croquet?"

The Tweedles stopped their arguing, and their eyes settled on me. Even the Duchess and the Cook turned to me as if they'd just realized there was a stranger in their midst.

"And who is this?" the Duchess asked the Rabbit, jutting her pointed chin upward ever so slightly.

"Duchess," the Rabbit started. "This is Alice. She's a visitor from the upper world."

"Why is she so small? Aren't they much larger up there in the world of giants?" The Duchess glared at me with judgment.

Maybe I could kill her, too. I forced an angelic smile. "Shrinking potion," I said, as if potions were the most normal thing.

The Duchess nodded. "Of course."

"I have an invisibility potion, too," I said with a sly grin. "A cater-pillar gave it to me."

"Huh. Tut, tut, girl. Er, Alice," the Duchess said. "Eat."

The Cook disappeared into the kitchen while we ate quietly, the Tweedles throwing perturbed looks at one another because they hadn't resolved their argument. I wondered if I'd put an end to the dispute if I explained that in my world, we'd been to the moon, and it was made of neither cheese nor biscuits, but rock and dirt.

"Will you be joining us for croquet tomorrow at the Queen's palace, Alice?" the Duchess asked. The piglet in the chair next to her snorted, and she took an apple from one bowl and gave it to him. He promptly began eating it with gleeful soft snorts. "That's my Baby," she cooed.

I imagined the piglet on a slow turning spit, roasting over an open fire, a small smile playing on my lips. "I've never played croquet," I said.

"It's a simple game. We'll teach you," the Duchess said with a wave of her hand. Then she turned to the Tweedles. "And you two?"

"I cannot think of croquet when my brother knows nothing of the moon," Tweedledum said with a forlorn sigh.

The Rabbit remained silent. He had finished his cake and now munched on a bit of lettuce, merely glancing at whoever was speaking.

I cleared my throat. "I am most interested in the magic of Won-derland. How things appear from nowhere and small teacups become big. Or how things change without the use of potions."

"Many parts of Wonderland are magic," Tweedledum said, straightening his bow tie.

"The plants help create potions, yes, but what about the other wonders?" I asked.

"Wonderland isn't magic, just some of *the creatures* are magic," Tweedledee corrected his brother.

"If the plants are magic, then Wonderland is magic," Tweedledum started. Back and forth they went, arguing whether it was the creatures and plants, or all of Wonderland, that contained the magic.

I couldn't get a word in. Finally, the Duchess clapped her hands together. "Dear Alice, let's go for a stroll under the moonlight to walk off this tremendous feast." She rose.

Immediately, the Tweedles returned to their argument about the moon. I stood, eager to escape, and glanced at the Rabbit, who shrugged and kept eating. I followed the Duchess from the dining room, my ears thankful for a reprieve from the bickering Tweedles. Yes, they would definitely have to go. *The residents of Wonderland might even give me a medal or call me a hero for saving them from the brothers,* I mused.

The Duchess led me outside and down a path to a grand garden. The cool evening air, fragrant with the scent of blooming nightshades and other curious flowers, was inviting. As we walked along the winding paths, the Duchess said something unexpected. "You know, my dear," she said, linking her arm with mine, "one must always remember to butter one's shoes before a long journey. It prevents blisters, you see."

I nodded politely, though I couldn't quite see the logic in her words. She was just as mad as the rest of them. The only one who seemed sane was the Rabbit. "But what if the butter melts?" I asked, genuinely curious.

"Ah, that's the beauty of it!" the Duchess exclaimed, her eyes twinkling. "Melted butter makes the shoes ever so much more comfortable. And if you happen to slip, well, it's just an opportunity to practice your balance."

We passed a bed of particularly vibrant flowers, their petals glowing softly in the night. The Duchess paused to admire them, then continued, "And never forget, Alice, that a well-timed sneeze can solve most of life's problems. Why, just the other day, I sneezed and found myself in possession of a most delightful hat!"

I could feel my eyes widen. What sorcery was this? Sneezing brought on hats? Or was she merely insane and absurd, like most of this place? "But what if one doesn't need a hat?" I asked.

"Then you must sneeze again, of course," the Duchess replied matter-of-factly. "One must always be prepared to sneeze at a moment's notice. It's the secret to true happiness."

Well, I thought, *that explains all the pepper*. As we walked further, the garden seemed to grow more enchanting, with fireflies dancing in the air and the wind whispering through the trees, creating a soothing melody with their soft rustle of leaves. The Duchess stopped to pick a peculiar flower with petals shaped like tiny teacups.

"Now, Alice," she said, handing me the flower, "always remember to water your dreams with a teaspoon of nonsense. It's the only way they'll grow properly."

I took the flower with a tight smile. "What fascinating advice. Thank you, Duchess," I said. "I'll be sure to keep that in mind."

We returned to the house to find the Tweedles nose to nose. "Cheese!" one said.

"Biscuits," shouted the other.

The Duchess exhaled an exasperated sigh. "Tut, tut, gentlemen. It's time for cocoa and then bed. We all have an early day if we plan to make it to the palace grounds to play croquet with the Queen."

"I'm not going," Tweedledee said, crossing his arms over his chest.

"Neither am I," Tweedledum spat back, taking on the same stance as his brother.

"Very well, Alice and Rabbit will go with me," the Duchess said. "And Baby," she said, giving the piglet a scratch under the nose.

"I'm ever so tired," I said.

"Oh yes, you would be," the Duchess replied, snapping her fingers. "Oh, Cook, could you please show Alice to her room?"

The Cook appeared, wiped her hands on her apron, and then looked me up and down, nodding. "Come along."

I was led to an upstairs room with a window overlooking the garden we'd just been in. The Cook produced a nightgown. "Wear this and I'll wash your dress tonight and have it ready for you in the morning. You cannot go to the palace in that state," she said.

Glancing down at my dress, I expected to see blood spatter, but that wasn't the case. From what I could see, my dress was just as clean and blue and white as it always had been, but I wasn't going to protest. I had no ill will toward the Cook. She seemed relatively normal amid all the nonsensical personalities of Wonderland. After she left, I cleared my pockets of the potion and knife, and slipped into the nightgown, leaving my crumpled dress on the floor outside my bedroom door. Lying down on the bed, I decided to wait until the house fell silent before I ventured out to kill the Tweedles, but the Duchess was my ticket to see the Queen of Hearts. That was the only thing keeping her alive—for now.

I waited until the house went silent and all I could hear were the creaks of the settling house and the soft snores from the other rooms. Barefoot, I crept out of bed, the wooden floor feeling gleefully cool against the soles of my feet. Like a thief in the night, I slipped from my room with my knife in my hand and tiptoed down the hallway toward the other rooms. I knew that in one of them, those annoying brothers, who argued incessantly, were asleep. They had no idea I was coming to kill them in their blissful slumber.

Approaching the first door, I put my ear to it. Inside, I heard soft animal grunts, likely belonging to the Duchess's baby. Tiptoeing past that door, I approached the second, again placing my ear near the door. Men's snores sounded from the room. In horror, I realized I'd forgotten my invisibility potion. It was no bother though. I could sneak in, cut one's throat while stifling any noise with my hand, or a pillow, then do the same to the other. A slow smile slid over my lips. Yes, that would do. And if I were caught, I'd have no choice but to eliminate all of them who came running, in which case I'd have to rely on the Rabbit to get me near the Queen.

I put my hands on the doorknob and turned it, delighted when it didn't make a sound. The door opened soundlessly without effort, and I slipped into the room and silently closed it behind me. Moonlight filled the room from a single window, giving me enough light to see what I needed to. On each side of the window sat a bed, and in each bed, the covered lumps of the Tweedles. I didn't care which was which, as they were both equally absurd. Now, each snored loudly. I found a decorative cushion on a chair to my right and snatched it up, then turned to the beds of the still slumbering men, deciding which one to remove from this world first.

The Tweedle in the closest bed was the first to go. Grasping my knife firmly, I eyed his jugular and, with my left hand, poised the pillow over his face. I waited for an exhale, then plunged the knife into his fat neck and sawed the blade through his flesh while simultaneously pushing the pillow down over his nose and mouth. The blood spurted out across my hand and wrist, warm and slick. I inhaled the scent of it. His body twitched and he brought his hands up, but just as quickly as they rose, they fell. Then his body tensed, and I heard a slight gurgle before he finally went limp and silent. I withdrew the knife, but held the pillow in place for another minute. Once I was sure he was dead, I inhaled—my heart thrumming in my chest and pounding in my ears. Pulling away the pillow, I found his eyes wide open, staring into the great beyond. I turned to the second bed.

The second Tweedle struggled fiercely, scratching at my arm and attempting to scream through the pillow. He managed to push the pillow away for a second and gasp, "Dum! Dum! Help me!"

Shifting his weight, he almost managed to get his feet on the floor, but I shoved the pillow back over his face and pushed hard to thwart all the noise, throwing my entire weight onto him, hoping the commotion didn't wake the entire household. Steadying my knife, I struck, only nicking his pale skin.

A muffled cry came from behind the pillow. "Why are you doing this? Why?"

"Because you and your brother are absurd and annoying, all you do is argue, and no one likes either of you," I said with a laugh. There was something pleasurable in being mean.

"But the moon really is made of cheese," came his muffled reply.

Throwing my full weight into him again, I made a swift strike to his jugular—this time with success. The blood spurted out over my fingers, seeping into the bedding. His thrashing slowed. I could hear him calling out into the pillow, "Dum, Dum." I pushed the pillow tighter against his face for another agonizing minute before his body went from rigid to limp. I removed the pillow carefully, revealing the terror in his lifeless eyes and gaping mouth. I got off of him, my muscles screaming with fatigue. I would be bruised by this kill. The Tweedles, being much larger than I, were a bit stronger, but not strong enough. While normally I wouldn't have found killing someone in their sleep a challenge, the second Tweedle did prove to be more of a match, much like the Hatter.

Wiping the knife on the pillow I'd used to muffle their cries and limit their air, I went to the window and looked down. Disposing of the bodies felt like a good idea. After all, the Duchess was needed, and I could use the invisibility potion to murder the Queen. With a nod to my plan, I opened the window and dropped the pillow to the ground below. Then, I carefully wrapped each Tweedle in a sheet and dragged them gently from their beds with the odd thump here and there, cringing each time I made too much noise. One by one, I wrestled their bodies to the window ledge and shoved them out, still wrapped in their blood-soaked sheets.

Each of them fell to the ground with a thump. When I was finished, I wiped my hands on the underside of one of the bed's blankets, then pulled the blanket up to cover the bloodstains. I pulled up the blanket on the second bed, too, using the underside to wipe away a bit of blood spatter on the wall. There in the moonlight, I looked down at my nightgown, noting it also had some blood splatter on it. Perhaps I could rinse it out when I washed up or hide it beneath the pillow when I dressed in the morning. Regardless, I needed to drag the bodies into the forest in hopes that Wonderland worked much the same as my world above, where creatures and insects would consume the flesh of the dead, leaving only bones for other animals to drag away and chew on.

I left the room as silently as I'd entered and tiptoed down the stairs and out the front door. One by one, barefoot and still wearing the blood-spattered nightgown, I dragged the corpses of the Tweedles into the dark woods.

THE WHITE RABBIT

I FOUND THE CAT sleeping next to the last embers of the fire in the
Duchess's sitting room. Not bothering to be quiet about it, I sat down
in front of him and waited for him to open his bright yellow eyes, so
striking that it was like watching two suns appear from behind furry
eyelids.

There was no point dancing around the subject with niceties and
formality. "Why did you have the Caterpillar give her an invisibility
potion?"

"Is that what it was?" There was a malevolent twinkle in the
Cheshire Cat's eyes.

"What was it?"

"What fun is that?" he asked. Then the grin, the one that stretched
to the moon and back, slipped from his face. "What about the Tweedles?"

Just as he said it, there was a 'thunk' outside the window. The cat
and I crept up to the sill and peered out into the darkness beyond. It
looked like a large white sack of some sort had been thrown from a
window upstairs. Then, from above us, we heard what sounded like
dragging, and then a long pause before another large sack fell from the

window above, landing on the first with that same 'thunk'. It took me a few minutes before I realized what we were looking at. The sacks were, in fact, bloodstained sheets, and their contents were no longer a mystery.

"There are your Tweedles," I said.

For the slightest second, I could swear the Cheshire Cat, with his ever-present smile, had a glint of fear in those solar orbs of his. And in a blink—he vanished before my eyes.

I wasn't sure what to do. Should I help Alice hide the bodies? Or was it more prudent to attempt to sleep and not know what became of the brothers? The latter seemed preferable. So, I went back to the small bed the Duchess had provided me in a corner of the sitting room and closed my eyes. As I did, I heard someone, likely Alice, come down the stairs and slip out the front door, and I listened as the lifeless Tweedles, one by one, were dragged away from the house and into the forest where their corpses would rot and decompose. Wonderland felt even more tainted.

I don't remember how long I sat there, my ears quivering in fear, but I must have exhausted myself because I somehow fell asleep. It was the nudge from Baby's snout and the voice of the Duchess from the kitchen that woke me up. "It seems the Tweedles left early this morning and won't be joining us for croquet. Tut-tut," she said to the Cook.

The Cook murmured something inaudible. That's when Alice entered the sitting room, fully dressed in her now perfectly clean and pressed blue and white dress. She'd put her hair in pigtails with deep blue ribbons tied into bows. Even her black shoes looked as though they'd been polished.

"Wake up, Rabbit," she said, a cheery grin on her smooth face. Then she rubbed her hands together with anticipation. "It's almost time for croquet at the palace."

I frowned. Alice had no idea just who she would be dealing with. The Queen was notorious for putting the residents of Wonderland on death row. Some she reprieved. Others, well, they simply disappeared. Alice, if she was going to rid us of the foul-tempered Queen of Hearts, would need to be strategic. "We should talk before we go. You'll need to have a plan, or the Queen will have you beheaded," I whispered.

Alice rolled her eyes and said, rather flippantly, "Yes, of course."

That's when the Cook called us all to the dining room for a rather excessive breakfast. Once we all sat, and Baby sat in the chair next to the Duchess, the Duchess tapped her glass with a fork. "Undoubtedly, the Queen will have tea and tarts, but you should never have more than one cup of tea and one tart on the palace lawn unless you want to be seen as a bad croquet player. The tarts weigh you down, you see. It's by design."

Alice glanced at me with the strangest expression. *We're all mad here*, I thought, and I think maybe Alice was thinking the same thing. In that moment, she gave the impression that maybe she wasn't too keen on Wonderland and all its odd inhabitants after all.

"So, fill your stomach now and our journey to the castle will lighten them!"

The Duchess reached out and took two yellow cupcakes from a bright green plate, handing one to Baby and stuffing the other, in full, into her mouth.

We dove into the cornucopia of cakes and cookies in silence, no one mentioning the Tweedles at first, but then Alice brought them up and I held my breath.

"Where are the brothers? What were their names again?"

Diplomatic, I thought. Alice was probably right to do this, though, because surely it would have been strange if no one had acknowledged their absence at all.

"Ah, the Tweedles. Forever arguing those two. I'm surprised they haven't spontaneously turned into mushrooms from all their disputing!" The Duchess waved her hand as if it was inevitable. "They've gone, probably to their cottage in the backwoods amongst the Jabberwockies, who stay away because they likely hate the sound of constant bickering."

"So, they won't be joining us?" Alice asked, as if seeking clarification, her big blue eyes feigning innocence.

"No, no. They annoy the Queen anyway. She's ordered their decapitation many times, only to later give them reprieve." The Duchess shoved a pink muffin into her mouth while setting another in front of Baby. The piglet ate, leaving a cascade of rainbow crumbs on the chair and on the floor beneath it.

We finished our breakfast, said goodbye to the Cook, and left the Duchess's house to walk to the castle. In my mind, I imagined the Cook going upstairs to straighten the rooms, only to discover the bloodbath, for surely with as much blood as I'd seen on those sheets, there was no way the room would be clean. I shuddered from ear tip to tail, realizing no one would be there to hear the Cook's screams. Would she race to the castle in a panic? Would she faint? Shaking the thought from my head, I hopped along behind the Duchess and Alice, turning my attention to their conversation.

"Why, my dear, croquet is as simple as buttering a hedgehog on a Tuesday! You see, you must always remember to keep your flamingo well-fed, for a hungry mallet is a grumpy mallet. And never, ever, let your hedgehog roll uphill on a Wednesday, for that would be quite the catastrophe! The trick, you see, is to aim for the wickets as if they were the Queen's tarts—deliciously elusive and ever so slightly mischievous. And if you find yourself in a muddle, just recite the Jabberwocky backwards; it works wonders for one's aim!"

"Uh, okay," Alice said, forcing a wide grin. "Do you play croquet with the Queen often?"

The Duchess shrugged, giving Baby, who she now pushed in a stroller, a quick glance. "Oh, often enough," she said. Then she turned to Alice with a serious expression. "Have you ever met a queen, my dear Alice?"

"No, ma'am," Alice said, pretending innocence again. The addition of *ma'am*, I thought, was a nice touch.

"My dear Alice, when it comes to the Queen, you must always re-member to curtsy with your left foot while balancing a teacup on your head—it's the only way to ensure she doesn't mistake you for a dodo! Speak to her as if you're reciting a riddle wrapped in a gossamer cloak, for she adores a good puzzle. And never forget, if she shouts 'Off with their heads!', simply offer her a slice of treacle tart; it works wonders for her temper. Above all, treat her with the same care you would a particularly prickly porcupine—gently, but with a firm hand!"

"A teacup?" Alice frowned.

The Duchess nodded emphatically. "Ah, Alice, the teacup is the secret to a perfect curtsy! You see, balancing a teacup on your head shows the Queen that you have grace, poise, and a steady hand—all qualities she admires. It also serves as a delightful distraction; while she's marveling at your balancing act, she might just forget to shout 'Off with their heads!' And, of course, it adds a touch of whimsy to the proceedings, which is always appreciated in Wonderland. So, my dear, keep that teacup steady and your head held high!"

"Does she often shout 'off with their heads'?" Alice's eyes nar-rowed, and I wondered if she was rethinking killing the Queen.

The Duchess threw her right hand back flippantly. "Oh, quite often, my dear! The Queen has a fondness for dramatic declarations. It's her way of keeping everyone on their toes, you see. But don't fret too much; most of the time, it's all bluster and no bite. Just remember to keep your wits about you and a slice of treacle tart handy—it's amazing how a bit of sweetness can temper even the fiercest of tempers!"

Alice glanced back at me, then back to the Duchess. "And which teacup should I use to balance on my head when I curtsy? The one I'm drinking from, or do I just randomly grab one from a table? What if there are no teacups?"

"Ah, Alice, such thoughtful questions! The choice of teacup is quite important, you see. If you're already drinking from one, by all means, use that—it shows resourcefulness. However, if you find a particularly charming teacup on a table, feel free to borrow it for the occasion. As for the dreadful scenario of no teacups at all, well, that's where your imagination comes in! Simply *pretend* you have the finest porcelain balanced atop your head. The Queen will be none the wiser, and you'll still make a splendid impression. Remember, it's all about the spirit of the thing!" The Duchess smiled with a satisfied nod at her own answer.

The conversation quieted as Alice thought about this and I was happy for the silence, but it was short-lived.

"Have you heard that the March Hare found the Mad Hatter slaughtered?" came a voice from the bed of flowers to the right. I stopped dead in my tracks.

Alice jumped. "What?"

The Duchess's hand went to her chest. "What?" she repeated Alice's question.

"The March Hare was late to the tea party, but when he arrived, he found a mess, and no sign of the Hatter, so he went into the garden and there he was. He'd been butchered," declared a lone sunflower.

The Duchess shook her head. "Oh, my stars and garters! The Mad Hatter, murdered? How utterly preposterous! Why, he's as resilient as a rubber teapot! Are you quite certain, dear flowers? Perhaps he's merely misplaced his head again—he does have a habit of losing things, you know." Then she peered down at the flowers. "Besides, how do you know?"

"The March Hare told me," said a daisy.

"The Cheshire Cat told me," said a petunia.

"Oh goodness me," the Duchess said with a sigh. "Perhaps we should make haste to the Hatter's and solve this crime."

Alice's eyes showed a hint of panic. "Well," she started carefully, "it makes sense that maybe, if news has already spread, and if the Queen is having her croquet party, that everyone is at the palace and we can discuss it there. Besides, isn't that a matter for the police? Or the Queen's guards?"

The Duchess nodded thoughtfully. "You have a point, Alice. The Queen's guards are quite adept at handling such matters, though they do tend to be a bit heavy-handed. But we can't just sit idly by, can we? We must at least gather some clues that we can present to the Queen."

"No, we should head to the croquet party and let the guards do their job," Alice said reassuringly. "They don't need us getting underfoot."

With a heavy sigh, the Duchess relented. "Of course you're right, my dear. I simply feel so helpless." Then her eyes widened. "I do know who might have some insight, though. Imagine if we went to the Queen with clues." The Duchess wasn't going to drop it.

Alice did a good job of holding back her annoyance. "Yes?"

"The Cheshire Cat. That cat sees everything and knows what's going on. I imagine the Cat knows who the murderer is!" She began purposefully pushing the carriage faster, leaving me and Alice no choice but to follow.

Behind us, the flowers whispered among themselves.

I could tell Alice was nervous. "A cat?"

"Not just any cat," the Duchess said. "The Cheshire Cat."

"What's the difference?" Alice asked.

I was glad I wasn't part of the conversation, but I felt this fresh development was leading us closer to the end of this dismal chapter for Wonderland, and the Cheshire Cat's oath to rid us of Alice.

"Ah, Alice, the difference is as clear as a teapot in a tempest! A regular cat, you see, is quite content with purring and chasing after mice. They are delightful creatures, but rather predictable. The Cheshire Cat, on the other hand, is a marvel of mystery and mischief! He can appear and disappear at will, leaving nothing but his grin behind. He's full of riddles and always seems to know more than he lets on. While a regular cat might curl up in your lap, the Cheshire Cat will curl up in your thoughts, leaving you pondering his words long after he's vanished. It's the magic of Wonderland, my dear!" She smiled kindly, but picked up her pace and I knew where we were going. There was a garden near the Queen's castle, where the Cheshire Cat was known to sun himself for several hours a day.

I knew better though. The cat was always watching, always grinning. Yet, he would appear if only to see Alice up close instead of from a distance. After all, with his magic, he'd be safe.

Alice, singularly minded, latched on to one small bit of information amidst everything the Duchess had just said. "How does one go about getting or learning this magic of Wonderland?"

The Duchess chuckled warmly, her eyes twinkling with mischief. "Ah, Alice, the magic of Wonderland isn't something you can simply learn, like a recipe for plum pudding. It's more about embracing the unexpected and seeing the world through a lens of unconventionality and wonder. You must be willing to believe in the impossible and delight in the absurd." She paused and turned to Alice. "Start by asking questions that have no answers, and always be ready to find joy in the most peculiar places. The magic is in the way you look at things, my dear. It's in the way you laugh at a riddle, dance with a shadow, or converse with a flower. Wonderland's magic is all around you, waiting to be discovered. All you need is a curious heart and an open mind."

There is none of that in Alice, I thought. No. Nothing but an icy heart and darkness. I found the words of the Duchess reassuring because it meant that Alice, no matter how hard she tried, could not grasp the magic of Wonderland for her own use unless it came to her in the form of a potion. I kicked myself once again for bringing her here and giving her the shrinking potion to save my own skin. Now, I regretted it deeply. The minute anyone discovered it was me who had unleashed Alice, I would either be banished from Wonderland and left to my fate above, or the Queen would have me beheaded. Either way, I would atone.

Alice seemed stymied by this revelation, likely because she knew now that there was no magic in Wonderland for her beyond the few potions she could get her hands on. I swallowed the lump in my throat and simply followed in silence, the whole of Wonderland turning gray and foreign all around me. As the color drained from everything, so did my optimism. The Cheshire Cat was our only hope.

ALICE

I WAS ALWAYS MORE of a dog person. While I never minded cats, there was something about them that made me nervous, and this was amplified when I first met the Cheshire Cat. The Duchess had led us to a beautiful garden full of many flowers—though these didn't talk, thank goodness. The longer I stayed in Wonderland, the more I began questioning my sanity. Imagine that. Me, a murderess rivaling the likes of Jack the Ripper, questioning my sanity. Ha!

But this cat was something entirely different, like something from one of the horror films my sister enjoyed watching. The Cheshire Cat was a most unsettling creature. As we stood in the middle of the garden, in front of us, above a tree branch, appeared a grin out of nowhere. It just floated in the air for a few moments before the rest of his body materialized, sitting on a branch. An icy shiver ran down my spine. His golden eyes glanced at the Duchess and the White Rabbit, then at me. He looked me up and down, his eyes appearing to pierce right through me, as if he knew all my dark secrets. Maybe he did.

The Duchess, with a mix of urgency and curiosity, approached the Cat. "Cheshire Cat, we need your help. The Mad Hatter has been murdered, and we must find out who did it. Do you know anything about this dreadful affair?"

The Cheshire Cat's grin widened, and he slowly faded in and out of sight. "Oh, Duchess, such a curious case indeed. The answer lies in the hands of one who holds a heart yet wears a mask of innocence."

I felt another chill run down my spine as the Cheshire Cat's eyes seemed to fixate on me. "What do you mean?" I asked, unable to control the slight tremble in my voice.

The Cat's grin remained, but his eyes sparkled with mischief. "In a land where logic bends, the truth is often hidden in plain sight. Seek the one who dances with shadows and speaks in riddles."

The Duchess, sensing the tension, looked between me and the Cheshire Cat. "What you say makes no sense!" She threw up her hands.

The Cheshire Cat vanished completely, leaving only his voice lingering in the air. "The answer you seek is both near and far, as clear as day and as murky as night. Look within and without, for the truth is a many-faceted gem."

When the Duchess's eyes fell on me, I merely shrugged, then rubbed the chill from my arms. The Cat was weird and creepy. "Does he always speak in riddles and then vanish like that when you need answers, leaving you more lost than before?"

The Duchess threw her hands up again. "Maybe Alice is right. We should just go to the croquet game and let the guards deal with this sad, sad event." A forlorn sigh escaped her lips.

I breathed a sigh of relief. There was no way I was a suspect. Yet. And once I became one, if I needed to escape Wonderland, I had the White Rabbit on my side. Through all of this, he had been a wonderful guide, even though I knew it was likely out of fear for his life and not loyalty or friendship. I was okay with that.

As I followed the Duchess and Baby from the garden, the White Rabbit lagging behind, I began musing on the strange Cheshire Cat and at how eerie it was the way he appeared and disappeared at will. It made me wonder if he was ever truly gone. Or was he always watching and waiting? Had he been there when I killed the Rat? When I killed the Hatter? Or the Tweedles? If he was, was this cat planning on stopping me? Or did he simply watch and do nothing?

With a frown, I realized there could come a time when I might have to kill the Cheshire Cat, too. If I could get my hands on him. We continued toward the palace. The surrounding woods pulsated with a life of their own, the gnarled trees contorting into grotesque shapes as if to mock our progress. But I strode forward, undeterred. Soon, I would face the Queen. The thrill of a promised hunt surged within me, a tide that could not be stemmed. Anticipation knotted in my stomach. Or was it fear? Maybe I was in over my head.

"Almost there," I murmured to no one, not really knowing if we were close or not. Each step brought us closer to impending madness, a prelude to the climax I so craved. Or at least I think I craved it. The bloodlust, the anger, it almost felt like it was vanishing, and, in that moment, I felt confusion and loneliness, even among the creatures of this strange land.

I turned to the Rabbit who looked a little tired. "Did you sleep well last night, Rabbit?"

The White Rabbit looked at me. "I slept well enough," he said.

This remained for us. Small talk. The Duchess, with long strides, seemed focused on reaching the Queen's croquet lawn and finding out who killed the Hatter, and the Rabbit had nothing to say. I had to break this lonely silence and the prison of my own thoughts. The only way to do that was to start a conversation, but how?

"I think after croquet and meeting the Queen..." I patted my dress pocket to make sure my knife and invisibility potion were there. They were. "I should probably return home." That's when a pang of homesickness hit me. I'd spent so much time in Wonderland that I was ready to return to my world. To my overly attentive mother and my sister. A pang of pain hit me in the chest, and I felt tears well up in my eyes. I fought them back. I would not allow myself to be a weak child. I was strong. I would destroy. The anger replaced the pain. Yes. Now I could kill the Queen. It would all end with the Queen.

The Duchess looked at me with a mixture of surprise and understanding. "Leave Wonderland, my dear? But why, when there's so much more to explore and discover?"

"Oh?" I asked, dabbing my eyes, very aware that the tone in my voice wasn't as enthusiastic as one might expect of a traveler from the upper world.

"Oh, my dear, there's so much more to see and do! Have you met the Mock Turtle and the Gryphon? They have the most delightful stories and dances. And then there's the Caterpillar, who sits atop his mushroom with his pipe and offers the wisest, if somewhat cryptic, advice."

"I met the Caterpillar," I said, once again absentmindedly patting the potion in my pocket.

"Don't forget the Mad Hatter and the March Hare's tea party..." She stopped herself and frowned, then let out another sad sigh. "Well, I suppose they'll be the March Hare's tea parties from now on, though I doubt it will continue to be an endless celebration of nonsense and riddles. Then, you've met the Tweedle Twins, Tweedledee and Tweedledum. They are always up for a bit of poetry and a friendly argument. You've met the Garden of Talking Flowers, where each bloom has a personality as bright as its petals." She paused to look at me.

I forced a smile.

That was enough to get her to continue. "There's also the mysterious Jabberwocky, a creature of legend and lore, and the ever-elusive Bandersnatch. You've met the Cheshire Cat, of course. Anyhow, Wonderland is a place where every corner holds a new adventure, and every moment is filled with fascination." She smiled. "So, before you decide to leave, why not take a little more time to explore? You never know what magical experiences await you just around the bend."

"I have a family back home," I said, and the words sounded distant, foreign, and even unfriendly. A family. What was that? A dead father? A distant sister, and an over-protective mother? Was that a family? The pain in my chest returned. My heart hurt and I wanted nothing more than to bury that pain in anger. *Kill, kill, kill*, I shouted in my mind. My stomach twisted. I was homesick, even if home was miserable. But then, I visualized myself going back down the rabbit hole and focused on where I was—here in Wonderland. That other world, the source of my despair, didn't matter here.

"Oh, my dear Alice, feeling a bit like a lost teacup in a tempest, are we? Homesickness is such a peculiar creature, isn't it? It sneaks up on you. But fret not, for in Wonderland, we have a remedy for every ailment, even the ones that tug at the heartstrings."

I threw her a smile as her words did not make me feel any better. "Everything here is so strange and confusing."

The Duchess nodded and continued to amble along the path, Baby snoozing in the pram. "Ah, but that's the beauty of it, my sweet! Strange and confusing are just fancy words for 'adventure' and 'discovery'." Then she stopped and whirled around to face me, her eyes wide as if she'd just remembered something extremely important. "Why, just the other day, I found a spoon that sings opera! Imagine that! And who knows, perhaps your home is just a hop, skip, and a rabbit hole away. Until then, let's make the most of our afternoon with the Queen."

I suppose that was her way of telling me to quit complaining. My sister might have told me the same. I rolled my eyes and let out a heavy sigh. At least the Duchess had stopped going on and on about finding the Hatter's killer. I didn't hate the Duchess, and I had no desire to harm her, but if she got in the way, I'd have no choice. I paused a little to let the Duchess go ahead and so the White Rabbit could catch up. "You must be tired," I said.

"So must you," he replied.

I shrugged. "Maybe once I finish hunting the prey I came to hunt, we can have tea and tarts, and then I'll return home. At least for a while." I glanced at the Rabbit to see his reaction.

His face remained passive. His ears and nose didn't react, and even his poof tail didn't move. We walked in silence for a bit, but then, the forest opened up to a grand lawn with ancient trees scattered about. Before us, an imposing stone castle dominated the landscape. It took me a few seconds to take it all in. I was in such shock that I didn't realize I'd stopped in my tracks.

"Come along," the Duchess called back.

I followed, unable to help but feel a mix of awe and trepidation. The path before us stood lined with rose bushes, some of which were being frantically painted red by a group of card soldiers. By cards, I mean they appeared to be actual laminated paper playing cards with arms, legs, and heads. I gave the strange creatures a wide berth but kept them in my peripheral view. Staring at them or asking the Duchess about them seemed impolite, so I kept my mouth shut and wondered how easy they were to kill. Their nervous glances and hurried strokes made me question what would happen if the Queen discovered a single white petal.

I hurried alongside the Duchess and asked in a mere whisper, "Why are they painting the roses red? Wouldn't it have just been easier to plant red roses?"

"Ah, my dear Alice, you see, in Wonderland, we have a penchant for doing things the roundabout way. Planting red roses would indeed be simpler, but where's the fun in that? Painting them adds a dash of exhilaration, a sprinkle of chaos, and a whole lot of character! Besides, the Queen does so love to keep her subjects on their toes."

I accepted her response, even though she was beginning to sound more and more like she was on Wonderland's tourism board. I smirked at my own observation but held my tongue. Then I noticed a strange feature to the castle itself. Each window, flag, and archway was shaped like a heart. Even the stone walls had heart patterns etched into them, and the turrets were topped with heart-shaped pennants that fluttered in the breeze.

As we drew closer, I noticed the grand entrance, guarded by more of the strange card soldiers standing at rigid attention. The massive heart-shaped doors were painted a striking red, with golden handles that glinted in the sunlight. Above the entrance, a large banner proclaimed, *Welcome to the Realm of Hearts*, in elaborate, swirling script.

I frowned. I wanted more answers about the paper-thin card men, and I almost asked the Duchess or the White Rabbit about this, but again, thought better of it. The Duchess would merely give me another *Wonderland is amazing* pep talk, and the White Rabbit, well, I wasn't sure what the Rabbit would say since he rarely said much. As we approached, the soldiers opened the doors and we walked past them, through the heart arch, and into the courtyard.

The courtyard was a hive of activity. More card soldiers marched in formation, while others tended to the gardens or polished the heart-shaped statues scattered about. In the center of the courtyard stood a grand fountain, its waters sparkling and cascading in the shape of a heart. One thing was certain, the Queen was obsessed with hearts, kind of like my grandmother had been obsessed with Hummel figurines and every surface in her home was covered in them. This reminded me of that—only more obsessive.

As I inhaled, my stomach growled with hunger. The air was filled with the delightful scent of freshly baked tarts, and in the distance, I could hear the clinking of croquet mallets and the occasional shout of "Off with their heads!" echoing through the grounds. It was a scene both strange and unsettling.

I just need to kill the Queen, I reminded myself.

As we approached the croquet field, I realized it was a chaotic patchwork of ridges and furrows, making it difficult to walk without stumbling. The croquet balls were live hedgehogs, curled up in defensive balls, their tiny eyes peeking out nervously. The mallets were equally bizarre—live flamingos, their long necks and legs making them awkward to handle. Each time a player swung a flamingo, it squawked indignantly, adding to the chaos of the scene.

I closed my eyes for a second and rubbed them, then opened them again, realizing the field was now a smooth lawn and the balls and croquet mallets were just that. Not a hedgehog or a flamingo in sight.

The Queen herself was in the center of it all, her face flushed with exuberance and fury. She shouted orders and threats with equal fervor, her voice carrying across the field. "Off with their heads!" she bellowed at the slightest provocation, her temper as unpredictable as the game itself.

"Why do people put up with it?" I half whispered, but the Duchess and the White Rabbit said nothing. As I watched this surreal spectacle, I couldn't help but question my mission. The absurdity of Wonderland was overwhelming, and the thought of returning home grew more appealing with each passing moment. Yet, the task at hand remained—ending the Queen. It was no wonder the White Rabbit had offered her up to my bloodlust, but could I really go through with it? The line between reality and madness blurred, and I found myself caught in the middle, unsure of my next move. I patted the knife and vial of invisibility potion in my pocket again for reassurance. "Curiouser and curiouser," I said.

The Duchess led us to the edge of the croquet field, and my eyes were drawn to an unexpected sight: another rabbit. The Duchess nodded, greeting the second rabbit with a smile. "March Hare, this is Alice. Alice, this is the March Hare."

The March Hare sat at a long, rickety table laden with an assortment of tarts. The table was a chaotic mess, with tarts of every imaginable flavor—strawberry, lemon, raspberry, and more—piled high on mismatched plates and platters. The Hare himself was a sight to behold. His fur was a wild tangle, sticking out in all directions as if he had just rolled out of bed. His eyes were wide and slightly manic, darting around as if expecting something—or someone—to appear at any moment. He wore a tattered waistcoat much like the White Rabbit's, but his pockets bulged with crumbs and bits of pastry.

He hunched over the table, one paw clutching a half-eaten tart, while the other gesticulated wildly as he muttered to himself. Every so often, he would take a large, enthusiastic bite, crumbs flying everywhere, and then pause to listen intently, as if the tarts themselves were whispering secrets to him. A few empty chairs surrounded the table, their cushions threadbare. The Duchess sat in one and pulled Baby from the pram.

Finally, the March Hare looked up, his eyes locking onto mine with an intensity that made me momentarily forget why I was here. "Ah, yes, hello, Alice. It's nice to meet you!" he exclaimed, his voice a mix of excitement and confusion. "Care for a tart? They're simply divine, you know. Freshly baked by the Queen's own pastry chefs, though I suspect they might be laced with a bit of madness."

"Off with their heads!" came a voice almost directly from behind me. I turned and found myself face to face with the Queen of Hearts. The Queen was a formidable figure, her presence commanding the attention of everyone in the court. Her face flushed with a perpetual look of indignation, and her eyes sparkled with a fierce intensity that made my heart race. Her regal attire was adorned with hearts, and her crown was perched precariously atop her red head of hair. Yet, there was something almost comical about her, as if she were a character from a deck of cards brought to life. Much like the strange card soldiers.

The Queen's eyes narrowed as she stared me down. With a dramatic flourish, she pointed her scepter at me. "Who is this?" she demanded, her voice echoing through the garden. "What is your name, child?"

I paused, feeling apprehension, then I remembered the Duchess' advice. Curtsy, as if I had a teacup on top of my head. I placed one foot behind the other and dipped at the knee politely. "Your Majesty, my name is Alice."

The Queen's expression softened slightly, and she gave an approving nod, but her tone remained commanding. "Well, Alice, you must understand that in my kingdom, everyone must follow the rules. And the first rule is to always obey the Queen!" She paused, her eyes gleaming with a hint of mischief. "Now, let us see if you can keep your head about you, young Alice. Welcome."

That's when something snapped inside me. *No, your majesty,* I thought. *Let's see if you can keep yours.*

THE WHITE RABBIT

ALICE SEEMED FINE ONE moment, like a normal girl. Then, something in her demeanor changed as she smiled at the Queen. I'm sure I was the only one who noticed, but then I'd seen Alice's insanity—the others had not.

The Duchess jumped up, curtsied politely, and greeted the Queen.

The Queen turned to us. "Hare, Rabbit," she acknowledged.

"Wasn't it the March Hare who found the Hatter?" The Duchess wasn't one to be shy. "The Cheshire Cat said your guards were dealing with the investigation."

"Yes! Such a shame. The Hatter was so entertaining…" The Queen's voice trailed off. "Come, eat tarts, play croquet. Today is not a day for sadness or investigations. I order you all to have fun or I'll have all of your heads!" With that, the Queen of Hearts strode back to the deep green croquet lawn and grabbed a mallet.

Soon, we were joined at the table of tarts by the Mock Turtle and the Gryphon. The Mock Turtle retelling another sad story and the Gryphon listening out of mere politeness. The Duchess introduced them to Alice who gave a few polite greetings before helping herself to some raspberry tarts.

The Mock Turtle, with his perpetually sad expression and slow, deliberate movements, always seemed to be on the verge of tears. His body was a curious mix of a turtle and a calf, with a shell that appeared rather worn and tired. He spoke in such a mournful tone, always reminiscing about his school days and the odd subjects he studied, like "Reeling" and "Writhing." It was enough to make anyone feel downcast.

And then there was the Gryphon, a creature of great strength and majesty, with the body of a lion and the wings and head of an eagle. He moved with such grace and confidence that I aspired to be like him, someday. His eyes sparkled with a mischievous glint, and he had a way of speaking that was both commanding and playful. He often teased the Mock Turtle, urging him to share more of his stories, which only made the Mock Turtle even more melancholic.

Together, they were an odd sight indeed, and I could tell they had entranced Alice, because she listened intently and watched them like a hawk. The Mock Turtle with his endless lamentations and the Gryphon with his boisterous energy. They seemed to balance each other out in the most peculiar way.

Alice finally turned to me, leaning into my ear. "What a strange pair. Have they been friends long?"

I nodded, wondering when and if she was going to do the deed and rid us of the Queen. Would she? Could she? It wasn't like I could ask without someone overhearing. Glancing at Alice again, I noticed she seemed lost in thought and out of place. Not just because she was a human girl, almost a woman, but because since being here her bloodlust seemed to come and go, like the tides of the ocean.

The Duchess soon joined the Queen in playing croquet. "Will you join them?" I asked Alice.

"I've never played before," she said, glancing nervously at the croquet setup on the lawn. The wickets, balls, and croquet mallets had changed again. The balls back to hedgehogs, the mallets flamingos, and the wickets, cards with hands and feet that did somersaults and moved—sometimes to help the Queen win, and sometimes to foil the shot. "The equipment, it keeps changing from the real thing to animals and cards," she said, bewildered.

I waved a paw absently. "It's always like this," I said.

The croquet ground was chaos, with flamingos squawking and hedgehogs rolling about in every direction. The Queen of Hearts was in her element, barking orders and threatening anyone who dared to miss a shot. Alice, looking a bit overwhelmed by the chaos, seemed to be trying her best to keep up with the ever-changing rules of the game.

Suddenly, a hush fell over the crowd as a familiar figure strolled onto the field. My heart leapt into my throat. It was the Mad Hatter, looking as lively and eccentric as ever, despite the fact that I distinctly remembered Alice having killed him. The March Hare jumped up and hopped toward him with such speed. "You're alive! You're alive!"

"Of course I am. Don't be ridiculous." The Hatter's eyes went straight to Alice, and he glared at her.

Alice's face went pale.

But the Mad Hatter tipped his oversized hat to the Queen and gave a flamboyant bow. "Your Majesty."

"But... but I thought he was..." Alice stammered, barely a whisper, unable to finish her sentence.

The Hatter strode over to the table, leaned over Alice and took a tart from the tray.

"How are you alive?" Alice asked. This caused the Mock Turtle and the Gryphon to quiet themselves.

"Oh, that nonsense!" The Hatter waved a dismissive hand. "In Wonderland, such trivial matters are hardly worth mentioning. Now, where's the tea?"

The Queen of Hearts, who had been watching the scene unfold with a mixture of curiosity and irritation, stepped forward. "Hatter! How dare you interrupt my game! Off with his—"

"Now, now, Your Majesty," the Hatter interrupted and turned to her with a mischievous grin. "No need for such drastic measures. I'm here to join the fun! Besides, I brought my own flamingo." He produced a brightly colored flamingo from behind his back, which squawked indignantly.

The Queen, momentarily taken aback, narrowed her eyes but said nothing. The Gryphon and the Mock Turtle exchanged bewildered glances and got up to join the game.

Alice, still trying to wrap her mind around the impossibility of it all, turned to me in a panic. "Will the others...?"

I shrugged. "No one in Wonderland has ever died before that I recall." That's when it hit me: it was possible that none of us could die—ever. I would have lived even if Alice had killed me in the upper world. Had I known this, I wouldn't have brought her here. But our immortality was a new discovery as no one I'd ever known had died. I lifted an eyebrow, and from the corner of my eye, I saw the grin and the eyes, and the Cheshire Cat appeared on a heart-shaped bench, licking a paw.

If I'd only known that things were about to get weirder. Emerging from the edge of the garden, Tweedledee and Tweedledum waddled in, looking as alive and well as ever. Their round faces beamed with their usual mischievous grins, and they cast knowing glances at Alice, who I saw shiver for a second.

"What the hell..." Alice whispered to herself. "Not them too!"

The Tweedles approached the Queen with exaggerated politeness, bowing deeply in unison. "Your Majesty," they said together, their voices harmonizing in a peculiar way. "We are most honored to be invited to your splendid croquet party."

The Queen of Hearts gave them a look of approval. "Tweedledee, Tweedledum. Welcome! Take your places and join the game."

"Thank you, Your Majesty," Tweedledee said, his eyes twinkling with mischief.

"Yes, thank you indeed," echoed Tweedledum, casting another glance at Alice, who was still trying to comprehend their presence.

As the Tweedles took their positions, they continued to exchange sly looks with Alice, as if sharing a secret only they knew. The game resumed, with the Tweedles adding their own brand of chaos to the already tumultuous scene by using the flamingos as swords and jumping ropes, the birds squawking at one another. Hitting the ball appeared to be optional in the case of the Tweedles. Nonetheless, they played with an exuberance that bordered on the ridiculous, their antics causing both amusement and confusion among the other players.

Alice leaned into me. "I must go."

"Why?" I asked, finding myself slowly growing amused by this unexpected turn of events.

"I'll use the invisibility potion and slip away." She frowned. "How do I get out of here?"

I shrugged. I knew how to get her in and how to shrink her, but I didn't have a growing potion to make her big again. "You'll have to find the Caterpillar for that answer."

Alice turned back to the game. I could see her mind mulling over it all.

I stood, excused myself, and went to join the Cheshire Cat on the bench. "Did you know they would not die?" I asked.

The Cat's tail flicked lazily, and he tilted his head to one side. "Oh, my dear Rabbit," he purred, "in Wonderland, death is but a fleeting inconvenience. Here, the impossible is merely a suggestion, and the improbable is our daily bread."

He paused, his grin growing even wider. "Besides, what fun would it be if things stayed the same? The Tweedles, though annoying, are far too entertaining to be gone for good. Now, tell me, have you ever tried to catch a shadow? It's quite the delightful chase."

"Alice wants to leave," I told him. "Without killing the Queen," I added in a whisper.

"Good choice," the cat said. "She only needs to use the potion."

"The invisibility potion?" I asked.

The cat nodded. "It isn't invisibility, actually."

I nodded with understanding, having suspected that might be the case based on the Cat's earlier hints. "You got the caterpillar to lie?"

"I asked him to," the Cat said, his eyes narrowing. "The potion merely makes her big again, and it sends her back to the world above."

Then a frightful thought filled my mind. "If she knows we can't die, what if she keeps coming back to satiate her bloodlust?"

The cat's eyes narrowed. "Just watch."

I turned to the croquet game again, noticing people whispering among themselves, the Duchess clutching her pearls. Everyone, it seemed, knew now what Alice had done.

I turned back to the cat, only to find he'd teleported to the table of tarts where Alice sat with her head down and her hands in her lap. There was a sorrow about her I couldn't quite place. This was quite a different Alice from the bloodthirsty, angry Alice who'd wanted to kill me. Who had killed the Hatter and the Tweedles in cold blood.

The Queen's face turned a deep shade of red, and she pointed a trembling finger at Alice. "You! How dare you show your face here after what you've done!"

Alice looked up, taken aback. She stammered, "W-what do you mean, Your Majesty?"

I cringed at her feigned innocence, since I knew better. How stupid did this girl think the creatures of Wonderland were?

The Queen's voice boomed across the field. "You killed the Hatter, and the Tweedles?! Off with her head!"

A murmur of outrage went through the small crowd.

Tweedledee and Tweedledum, who had been playfully arguing over a hedgehog, turned to Alice with accusing eyes. "You killed us!" Tweedledee said, his voice trembling with anger. "We woke up in the forest covered in sheets. You made us late to the Queen's croquet party!"

"How could you?" Tweedledum added, his usual jovial expression replaced with one of betrayal.

The Gryphon and the Mock Turtle, who had been watching, stepped forward. "This is an outrage!" the Gryphon roared. "We trusted you, Alice!"

The Mock Turtle's eyes filled with tears. "Oh, the sorrow of it all! How could you bring such sadness to Wonderland?"

The Duchess merely gave Alice a look of disappointment.

Even the Cheshire Cat, who now sat at the table with Alice, managed a slight frown. "Tsk, tsk, Alice."

Alice seemed to panic then. "But... but they're here! They're alive! How can I have killed them?"

The Queen's eyes narrowed. "No excuses! You will pay for your crimes! Guards!"

In a flurry of what sounded like a thousand paper wings, and pebbles hitting stone, the guards started forward.

Alice caught my gaze, her eyes pleading with me to help her. "Run, Alice. Run while you still can," I said. But I knew it sounded sinister rather than sympathetic or urgent. I was enjoying this.

Without a second thought, Alice turned and fled from the table onto the lawn, the angry shouts of the guards, and the Queen's repeated declarations, "Off with her head!" echoing behind her. She darted through the garden.

"Stop her! Off with her head!" the Queen bellowed, her voice filled with rage.

Alice glanced over her shoulder, her breath coming in ragged gasps. The Gryphon's wings beat the air furiously, and the Mock Turtle's mournful wails added to the cacophony. The Cheshire Cat appeared and disappeared, his disapproving frown floating in the air.

Desperately, Alice scanned the garden for an escape. The card soldiers, with their spears raised, were closing in fast.

She thrust her hands into her dress pocket, producing the potion the Caterpillar had given her. Flicking the cork from the bottle, she drank it down just as one of the card soldiers thrust his spear into her side, the tip piercing her skin.

With a cry of pain, Alice fell backward.

The soldiers skidded to a halt as the girl vanished in a flash.

I worried then that the Queen would turn her wrath on me for bringing Alice here, but she did not. Instead, the Queen seemed to think I was on their side—I was. No one put the blame on me for bringing Alice to Wonderland. Nor did the Cheshire Cat rat me out.

I was thankful for both. At least now I knew Alice could never come back.

Then the Queen said something that chilled me to the bone. "Very well, then. We'll have to go to her world. Off with her head!"

"Off with her head!" came the chorus of chants from my friends. I followed suit and chanted along with them. The sooner we got this over with, the sooner life in Wonderland could get back to normal.

ALICE

THE WORLD AROUND ME began to blur and shift as the potion took effect. I felt myself growing rapidly; the spear slipping into my side becoming a mere sliver. I lay face down in the forest, but not the forest of Wonderland. The forest behind my house in my small town. I got to my feet and looked around, noticing the back of the garden shed in the distance. I hurried toward the house, toward my bedroom, because behind me I heard thumps in the forest as the characters of Wonderland entered my world. They must have had enlarging potions because the sound of their pursuit suggested they were my size or bigger.

"Off with her head!" I heard in the distance. They were coming. They were coming for me!

The White Rabbit's words echoed in my ears. *Run, Alice.* So, I ran. I made it to the house, sprinting up the back steps two at a time, across the porch and in through the back door.

"Alice?" I heard my mother call as I made it to my room and slammed the door closed behind me. Pulling my knife from my pock- et, I opened it, revealing the blade—small but effective. Something was sliding beneath the door. Paper of some sort. No, it was a soldier! A card soldier!

Leaping onto my bed, I held the knife in front of me. They were coming for me, and this time, in this world... I didn't have time to finish the thought. A card soldier slipped under my door as another came in from the open window. They kept coming, their spears much larger now. I thrust my knife forward, stabbing them over and over, fighting off their spears and tearing them in half. Luckily, they were paper, and my knife tore through them rather easily. Their blood and limbs scattered everywhere, turning the walls of my room red. In the distance, I heard a knock at my bedroom door. I heard someone shout my name, and I felt spears jabbing me from all sides.

There were too many of them. I sank down under the heap of card soldiers, succumbing to them, and knowing that soon, they would take me back into the woods, and even back to Wonderland, to en-act the Queen's orders. *Off with my head*, I thought just before the darkness took me.

I woke up fighting for my life. Two big men held me down. A third had a needle. I didn't know why the men in white were holding me down, but then I felt my flesh give way as the needle punctured my arm. A sudden rush of warmth washed over me and there was nothing I could do. I could see everything now—a moment of clarity so bright that the vibrant colors of the world assaulted my eyes.

I focused on my mother and my sister, standing to the left. My mother held a tattered copy of my favorite book in her hand, *Alice in Wonderland* by Lewis Carroll. The cover and pages were frayed from my constant re-reading. The spine was broken.

My sister's voice came to me, as clear as the White Rabbit's had, "Will Alice be okay, Mom?"

My mother nodded with tears in her eyes. "I hope so."

A man with dark hair and eyes, in a white lab coat, looked down at me. "How long has she been like this?"

My mother let out a shuddering breath. "Since this morning. She has been mumbling to herself. She tore up her room with the pocketknife her father, my late husband, gave her."

The man looked down at me with worried eyes. "It's going to be okay, Alice." Then he turned back to my mother just as the two men strapped me by my legs and ankles to the flat bed I lay upon. I couldn't move and suddenly, I began to feel sleepy. My bed began moving. "Help me! Help me!" I called, hoping the Queen and her card soldiers weren't still in pursuit.

My sister began crying and my mother put a reassuring arm around her.

"What is this?" the man asked.

"It's Alice's favorite book. Her father used to read it to her all the time. It was their thing." Big, wet tears fell from her eyes. She handed the book to the man. "Is it okay if she has it?"

"It might help." Then he took my mother's hand. "It seems your daughter, in her grief, has had a psychotic break," I heard the man say.

"How..." my mother sobbed. This time, my sister comforted her.

"It's going to be okay. Alice is in excellent hands. With time, and therapy, her prognosis is good," the man reassured them.

"But I've done everything right," I heard my mother say. "I put her in therapy. I've been working from home..."

"She was close to her father. It will take time," the man said, his voice growing fainter.

The bed beneath me began moving faster, away from my mom and sister. We went through a doorway and two pale beige doors swung closed behind us, and then it was just me and the two men, their faces melting, replaced by the bloodied faces of Tweedle Dee and Tweedle Dum with their dead eyes. "We're going to take good care of you, Alice," Tweedle Dum said, his eyes glinting with vengeful malice.

"Where is the Queen?" I asked, now terrified that they would do to me exactly as I did to them.

"The Queen will be by later to see you," Tweedle Dee assured me, glancing at his brother in a strange way that made little sense to my muddled mind.

My eyes felt heavier and the world around me turned gray. What sins I had committed, and now, what I'd done to them, they'd do to me. I began shrinking and falling, back down into that rabbit hole, The White Rabbit's laughter gleefully following me into the darkness. And that wicked smile of the Cheshire Cat mocked me as I fell into the abyss.

Twisted Tales of Familiar Faces

If you enjoyed this corrupted retelling of *Alice in Wonderland*, don't miss out on the rest of this horrifying collection!

Humbug (Scrooge) - Andre Gonzalez

Sweethaven (Popeye) - RJ Clark

Timber Beast (Paul Bunyan) - A.K. Hughey

Alice (Alice in Wonderland) - Audrey Brice

Wish (Aladdin) - Courtney Konstantin

Quixote (Don Quixote) - Stephen Wertzbaugher

Arturius (King Arthur) - A.K. Hughey

Steamboat (Steamboat Willie) - Courtney Konstantin

Strangled (Rapunzel) - Stephen Wertzbaugher

Dethroning Oz (Wizard of Oz) - Audrey Brice

Scorned (Hercules) - Z.S. Diamanti

Check out the entire collection at www.m4lpublishing.com

Join our newsletter to stay up to date with all upcoming releases at www.m4lpublishing.com

Author's Note

Thanks to M4L Publishing and Andre and Natasha for inviting me to participate in this project, and for working so diligently to bring it to life. You both are amazing.

Enjoy this book?

We hope you enjoyed this release from M4L Publishing.

Reviews are the most helpful tools in getting new readers for any books. We don't have the financial backing of a New York publishing house and can't afford to blast our books on billboards or bus stops.

(Not yet!)

That said, your honest review can go a long way in helping us reach new readers. If you've enjoyed this book, we'd be forever grateful if you could spend a couple minutes leaving it a review (it can be as short as you like) on the site you purchased this book from.

Thank you so much!

About the author

Audrey Brice writes award-winning dark fantasy, paranormal, urban fantasy, supernatural horror, and mystery novels. She also writes under three different pen names including Anne O'Connell, S. J. Reisner, and S. Connolly.

www.ingramcontent.com/pod-product-compliance
Lightning Source LLC
Chambersburg PA
CBHW030906200726
48289CB00003B/916